Potions and Panic

Astoria Wright

Faerie Apothecary Mysteries
Book 5

Potions and Panic

Copyright © 2019 by Astoria Wright

Published by Novelwright Press, LLC
http://www.novelwright.com

Cover Art by Viyiwi
www.fiverr.com/viyiwi

Editing by 529 Books
https://www.529books.com

Table of Contents

Chapter 1

Tempest in a Teacup

The field of flowers in First Street Park on a sunny spring day seemed like a perfect launching site for Cameron Larke's mayoral campaign—until the twister hit. As with most storms, it started with rain. At least the custom umbrellas with the slogan *"Happy as a Larke"* had found a use. Moss Hill's residents swiped the last of the promotional gifts as soon as the clouds conspired against them.

Carissa Shae snapped open her peach umbrella and raised the campaign catchphrase over her fiery red hair. Her new pink-striped dress whipped in the wind. *Of all the days to wear a short dress; if only Maren hadn't insisted the candidate's girlfriend had to be in style*, she mused to herself while Mossies, as she and the townsfolk called themselves, gathered around the raised, wooden platform.

Maren Raines, Carissa's friend and assistant, cursed as the wind played tug-of-war with her umbrella. While she wrestled with the clasp, the sky

1

took on an ill-omened shade. Carissa leaned in to help, but before she could offer any assistance, Maren gave it a violent yank.

"Blasted thing!" she exclaimed when it finally *popped*, nearly hitting the person in front of her. Her "sorry" was lost on the man, whose open-mouthed stare led Carissa to wonder how he'd never seen a storm before.

Chaos, the three-inch, tan-skinned nature faerie on Carissa's shoulder, pulled on Carissa's ear to show her concern for the safety of the tea and scones. The Gooseberry Bakery tent rippled with each gust of wind, but Carissa knew it would hold. She shushed the nature faerie.

Cameron Larke, near perfection in his handsome, gray, fitted suit, stepped confidently up to the podium. His crimson tie brought out fiery red tones in his cognac brown eyes that not even the cloudy weather could dim. Carissa and the others clapped loud enough to scare the thunder away.

"Thank you for coming out this morning. I thought the umbrellas might come in handy for the *afternoon* rain that was predicted. There might be a sylph or two up there showing their support."

Chuckles peppered the air. Only a Mossie would know about the elemental sky faeries who were said to rain blessings down on people. But sylphs were rarely sighted, even in Moss Hill, since they blended in with the clouds. Carissa laughed in surprise that Cameron would make a joke about the weather, given how nervous he'd been about it when they were setting up for the event. Instead of holding on to worry-filled what-ifs, he had been getting better at seeing silver linings these days.

Resting his gaze a moment longer on Carissa than anyone else, Cameron found each person's eyes as if he were speaking directly to them. Carissa felt the elf-light magic jumpstart her heart. Her human half struggled to contain the glowing pride that her fae side might literally unleash.

It wasn't just that he was acting mayor, soon to be elected for a full term. It was that he had long been her friend, her supporter, and her admirer. Here was a chance for her to be the same to for him.

Cameron's shoulders relaxed and the "Camera Cam" she so often teased him about disappeared, replaced by the easygoing man everyone loved. He pocketed his speech and set both hands on the podium.

The gentle drizzle became a steady drumbeat on the speakers. The wind whispered in Carissa's ears with the message of a storm brewing. Cameron's voice rose like a boat over waves.

"The weather seems to have taken a turn."

The forecast had said a possibility of *light* rain. Cameron and Carissa had hoped the rain might start after the speech. Sending everyone off with umbrellas would have been ideal, but they were prepared for this, too.

Cameron's eyes found Carissa again. She whispered, "Okay, now," to Chaos who, along with several over nature faeries, took to the sky. The crowd gasped as a moss-colored tarp unfolded from the ground to extend over all of their heads. With their magic in place, the sprites were free to fly above the Mossies' heads. Chaos opted to sit back on Carissa's shoulders. With the beautiful display, the rest of Cameron's message took on greater meaning.

"We have weathered a series of storms."

Tempests were more like it, with a banshee, a hobgoblin, a redcap, an attempt on the previous mayor's life, and a changeling invasion on top of it. Moss Hill had been attacked by more unseelie faeries in the last year than in all of its history, and she feared the evil faeries had even more in store for them.

"I know there's a lot of fear and doubt about the future," Cam continued, "but we, Mossies, fare better when we combine our strengths with those of our neighbors. With my candidacy, I propose friendship, loyalty, and unity over Moss Hill and Vale. If we have these things, we'll…."

Carissa missed the last part of what he said when a sharp pain pinched her right ear. Chaos mercilessly tugged it again. She clapped down on the lobe before the nature faerie could yank it a third time.

"Ow, stop that! The scones are fine," Carissa began to say.

But Chaos wasn't looking at the Gooseberry tent. She floated above Carissa's eyes, pointing upward. Rubbing her reddened earlobe, Carissa shot an upward glance at the sprite, ready to scold, but words were lost on her the next moment.

The nature faerie magic lost its tug-of-war with the wind. The tarp escaped into the wild. One by one the umbrellas popped back open as the Mossies were left to wonder why they were suddenly being soaked. Carissa frowned. The effect was less impressive than they'd planned.

What was worse, something strange was stirring in the sky. Dark clouds swirled clockwise. Having mastered the art of umbrella opening the second time around, Maren pushed a strand of light-brown hair out of her eyes and leaned toward Carissa.

"What's happening?"

Chaos flapped her red wings, lifting her just enough for them to see where she was pointing. Maren gasped. Carissa yelled for Cameron's attention.

"Look out!"

An alarmingly short distance behind the platform, black wind swirled at a quickening pace. Screams from the crowd drowned in the storm. The nature faeries fled—all except Chaos.

Cameron stopped mid-sentence. His rich brown hair danced wildly as he turned to face the phenomenon. It was too late to dash out of the way of the...*woman?* barreling toward them.

A thin woman in a black dress crashed onto the stage with enough force to knock Cameron into the lectern. The microphone gave a high-pitched shriek over the howling wind. Umbrellas dropped as Mossies clasped their hands over their ears.

But she was standing.

Her waist was cinched with buttons blending into the fabric so that only the gleam at certain angles revealed that they were there. It was an almost militaristic style, which fit her commanding presence.

The woman's umbrella had come undone by the force of the storm. *The storm that had brought her here.* Whatever kind of fae she was, she was powerful.

Carissa gripped her own umbrella tighter as the woman let go of hers and it disappeared. The wind died down. The black swirl turned to wisps. The drizzle stopped and gray skies parted to blue. The mysterious middle-aged woman combed her fingers through her long tresses as the twister dissipated.

Carissa couldn't see Cameron's face, but she imagined the shock was palpable. Fearless-in-the-face-of-danger was not his brand of heroism. But he stood and placed himself between the woman and the crowd. She spoke to him as if he was simply there to serve her.

"I'll take the microphone, please."

"Who are you?" Cameron's less-than-welcoming greeting evoked only mild disinterest.

"If I had the microphone, I could tell all of you at once. Now, I made a request kindly. I'd rather not make it a command, young man."

Her tone bordered on threatening, and she'd already proven that she had the power to back herself up. Well, Carissa had magic of her own. Unpracticed as it might be, she had more than elf-light magic, too. Carissa snapped her umbrella shut. She took a few steps toward the stage, but Chaos beat her to it.

The nature faerie bounced off Carissa's shoulder and raced past the astonished assembly up to the dark-haired woman. She circled around the stranger once, then did cartwheels on her shoulders. As her miniscule hands enveloped the woman's cheek, Chaos glowed like a firecracker.

"Yes, yes, I'm happy to see you, too," said the woman.

Recognition sparked. Of course, Chaos wouldn't see *her* as a stranger. Carissa stopped just before the stage. Movement followed behind her.

"Who is that?" Maren asked, sliding her spring lavender umbrella down slowly so as not to catch the woman's attention.

Carissa could not pull her eyes away from the sight of the stranger to whom Chaos was clinking. Without blinking, she responded, "Chaos knows her. Who else could it be?"

She had said she was coming. Carissa had shown the note to Maren months ago. It had arrived on the doorstep of Carissa Shae's natural pharmacy with a chocolate cosmos and a nature faerie and the prophetic warning: *Moss Hill is in danger.*

As the woman stepped up to the podium, waiting for Cameron to step aside, a twister of its own turned Carissa's stomach. She looked around. Mossies hung on to their hats and reporters clutched their notepads and cameras. Most Carissa knew well, like Tilly Brier, who was keeping herself collected enough to calmly snap pictures with her cell phone. Others, those whose eyes had grown wider than their camera lenses, were not familiar.

Tourists.

There weren't supposed to be tourists at this community event. Carissa and Cameron could explain away the dancing nature faeries and tarp as a magic trick, but a woman appearing in a twister? Whoever she was, why did she have to come through the human realm when she could've just as easily entered the island via the faerie realm? Seelie or unseelie, the fae never revealed themselves to humans of the outside world. They'd grown too comfortable with Moss Hill and its unique mix of humans with fae heritage and an open-mindedness to the Otherworld. More and more tourists had caught glimpses of magic over the last few months. Would they have camera images of fae magic now, too?

Chaos hopped down to throw enough faerie dust on the microphone for it to rise. It squealed again. The woman raised an eyebrow and the device whimpered, then stopped. She cleared her throat.

"That didn't quite go to plan. I'll have to do that more often for practice. This is for speaking into, right?"

Chaos nodded vigorously.

Raven leaned forward. "Good morning, Mossies! Your worries are over."

A boat horn blew in the marina behind her. Raven barely batted an eye. She did pause for it to stop, though.

"To clarify, there is still trouble to come for Moss Hill, but now that I'm here, you need not worry about it. As of this second, you are in my care."

"But who are you?" a woman asked from the crowd.

Carissa recognized Mrs. Harbridge, the business association manager and co-owner of Harbridges, the haberdashery. The boat horn blew again. This time mild annoyance graced the woman's face.

When the sound stopped, she said, "I am Raven Corvus."

The internal whirlwind pushed Carissa's heart into her throat. She swallowed. The next boat horn's blast felt like a warning:

Mossies: prepare to panic.

Chapter 2

The King's Ship

The final horn blast distracted Raven from whatever she might have said next. She disappeared in a cloud of black smoke, far less disruptive than a twister but just as intimidating.

A din began to rise from the crowd. Befuddled mumblings drowned out Cameron's message. The confused Mossies speculated as to who the woman was and how she meant to terrorize Moss Hill. Worse, what had she done to the incoming boat to cause its horn-blowing distress?

Cameron adjusted the microphone. The static pop snagged the people's attention. He cleared his throat.

"Please, remain calm. I know that was unusual, but—"

Another blast from the ship, this one long and threatening, caused another wave of tension to roll through the crowd. Cameron could no longer hold their attention as they turned to see what they could of the marina.

Some people bolted for their cars. Others bustled to the marina. Maren kept glancing toward the shore. Even Carissa wanted to see who had arrived, but she had to find Hiya and Cynth first.

The poor nature faeries had rushed off with the others, but they weren't wild fae who wandered the town alone. They'd still be nearby. She looked for signs of faerie dust in yellow and pink. Failing that, she looked for movement of little figures or tiny objects. A rattling teacup fit the description. She found them cowering in an empty floral print cup and saucer. They were still trembling when she scooped them into her hands.

"Go home," she said, "I'll see you there soon."

They looked at her, then each other, then back again. She coaxed them with a "go on, it'll be all right" before they finally moved.

Carissa looked around the park, searching for Cameron, but he was nowhere to be found. The thought occurred to her to also look for the pale, terror-stricken faces of tourists to put at ease later. She might have to persuade them that they had suffered hallucinations from bad shellfish or mold or whichever calamity would seem most plausible. The trouble was, everyone's face held the same shock – Mossies included. Raven's magic was beyond what a faerie could do. If Carissa had her suspicions before, she was now convinced that Raven was not a fae at all, but something more.

"It's the king's boat!" Maren had either overheard something or caught sight of something this far away to make out the identity of the vessel. "They weren't supposed to be here until this afternoon. I'm not even dressed cute!"

She pulled at her clothes and smoothed her hair. Maren, having worked the early shift at Gooseberry today, still wore the pink shirt and blue pants with the pie insignia and the lingering scent of cinnamon rolls.

Since her boyfriend, Reg, had journeyed to the home of the King of Sidhe and Elves four months ago, he was one of the passengers returning on the king's ship today. Reg would be glad to see Maren, however she looked. Carissa would have said something to reassure her, but Maren took off toward the marina.

Quickening her pace to keep up with Maren, Carissa felt her heart thudding in her chest. She had just as much reason to be upset at the boat's early arrival. She'd closed her shop only for the morning, planning to be at work when the ship arrived. Her parents had come and gone often enough that they did not need her to meet them at the marina. And if a certain prince her parents had tried to set her up with was on board, things might get awkward between her and Cameron.

She really needed things to not be awkward between them. Especially today with his parents joining them for lunch at her house. Was that still happening given the current situation?

Carissa stopped and looked back at the podium one last time. Putting one hand on her hip and one on her forehead, she looked this way and that. Still no Cameron. Now she'd lost Maren, too.

A hand caught her wrist. She spun around as if ready to take a swing.

"Whoa, Cari, it's me." Cameron held his hands up defensively.

Carissa dropped her fist and relaxed. Cameron stepped closer.

"Are you all right?"

His cognac eyes questioned her emerald-green ones. Of the two of them, she was the one with the magic, but she felt somehow safer with his arms enclosing her.

"I'm fine," she said. "Maren's somewhere ahead."

He let go. His eyes scanned the marina.

"There." He tilted his chin in the direction of the dock. "Wow, she really found her way to the front."

Carissa could make out one furiously waving figure being ushered back by a sidhe guard. Maren. The guards made an impassable barrier as they stood at attention on the dock. Had they been there during the whole commotion with Ms. Corvus?

It was worse than that. Tourists may not have distinguished Carissa's slightly pointed ears as being anything more than human, but the sidhe guards had even pointier ones, sharper eyes that changed color with their emotions, and uniforms that looked like they'd come from some alternate Victorian era. Intermixed in crowds, they might not garner attention, but guarding the unearthly boat, they were asking to be found out as fae.

Carissa and Cam made their way down, pushing through Mossies to join the sidhe and Maren. The boat slowed to a halt with a screeching sound. Carissa let go of Cameron's hand to shield her ears.

This wasn't a noise she expected from a fae boat. The tone may have been gentler in the Otherworld, but, like last time, the boat chose to enter in the human realm. Mossies threw up their hands in defense of their eardrums.

"Ugh," Maren moaned. Her painted paisley nails covered each of her temples. "Why do they have to blow the siren?"

The siren? That's what it was. When all was said and done, five short blasts had sounded.

Danger.

The boat settled at the dock. The gang plank assembled, but rather than a group of disembarking passengers coming down, the sidhe rushed up the wooden ramp.

"Something's wrong," Carissa stated.

Cameron nodded. "Wait here. I'll go and see what it is."

He took quick, decisive steps toward the gangway. Carissa rolled her eyes. Stay here? He had to know her better than that. And since when did he rush headfirst into danger?

"Hey," Maren said. "What's going on?"

Carissa looked up to the deck. She couldn't see anything. In the noise of the crowd, her elf ears couldn't pick up anything either.

"C'mon," she said. "Let's go find out."

A lower ranking sidhe guard stopped them right after allowing Cameron to pass. As interim Mayor of Moss Hill, he had some authority to enter. Aside from that, the captain of the sidhe guard, Varick, walked with him.

"Cameron," Carissa called.

He and Varick both turned. She matched the scowl on Varick's face and added an eyebrow raise to challenge. True, she and Maren had no official business on the ship, but there was no point in keeping Carissa out. She'd only find another way in and he'd have to face her wrath later.

"They are with me," Varick said.

The sidhe guard stepped aside. Maren couldn't move on without giving the guard a piece of her mind.

"You know, she's Carissa Shae—the one who stopped the changeling invasion on Valentine's Day. You're lucky to have her help."

"Okay, Maren." Carissa locked her elbow with Maren's and pulled her away before she could aggravate a sidhe more than was healthy for a human.

"I'm just saying that whatever is going on, you're more than able to help."

"I'm not sure that I am."

Carissa stopped in her tracks at the top of the gangway. Maren stopped, too. A circle of sidhe, elves, and a roguishly handsome man in black crouched around something at the bottom of a stairway to the upper decks. Beside them stood Raven Covrus.

"How does she do that?" Maren asked.

It was a good question. Raven seemed to have disappeared from the podium and reappeared directly on the ship. Given how she'd arrived in Moss Hill, it seemed safe to assume she could travel place to place instantaneously.

Carissa knew only one other person in Moss Hill who could disappear at will—and he was not a faerie. He was not alive, actually. The ankou, Moss Hill's Grim Reaper, was the only one powerful enough for even faeries to dread. Carissa doubted Raven had any fears.

She certainly didn't seem to be afraid of the corpse at her feet.

Carissa couldn't see clearly from the circle of guards blocking her view, but she thought she spied a woman lying on the floor. Raven walked once up and once down the woman's form. Finally, she stopped, and the elves parted enough for Carissa to see that there was, indeed, a red-haired victim on the floor. With her hands sprawled over her head, she looked as if she'd fallen—or been pushed—from the stairs.

Tapping her cheek, Raven said, "Hmm, that is a mystery. You—" She pointed to the man in black. "Are you the ankou?"

The man's eyes widened. "No, ma'am, I am not."

His Scottish accent made Carissa wonder about Raven's lack of one. Or rather, she tended to take on the accent of whomever she was talking to at the time. Now, it matched the man's voice.

"You're sure? Oh, well, it's a pity. We'll need him."

She placed her arms up similarly to the way Chaos had done whenever she called out to Alden. Carissa knew the sprite had the ability to summon the ankou, but could Raven do it so easily? And would she do so on a fae vessel? The sidhe, as immortals, especially didn't take well to ankous.

Cameron, who knew this and didn't know Raven well enough to leave the situation alone, walked toward her. Carissa tried to call him back. Why was he acting so brashly? He shouldn't try to stop a fae as powerful as her.

A storm of stomping heels clacked against the floor. Raven put down her hands. Macara rounded the corner with an elf in full regalia. It had to be the captain, considering his royal purple jacket with gold rank markings on the shoulders. The white vest and pants might have seemed outdated, but they were a radiant material that almost appeared to glow.

Carissa released a long, steady breath. It wasn't the prince. That, at least, was a relief. She could smile at Macara now.

"Sister," Raven said with a cheerful tone.

The word confirmed Carissa's suspicion. Since Miss Morgan's death, she'd discovered that the old woman was part of the Morrigan, a triple goddess figure to humans of old. One of the Tuatha de Danann, an ancient race predating the fae, Macara did seem godlike in her powers. And Raven was her sibling—the third of the Morrigan sisters.

"Nemain, or is it Raven now?"

Raven clucked her tongue. "I never liked Nemain. Raven is a good one, don't you think?"

"Don't *you* think coming back here right now is a bad idea?"

"I missed Chaos."

Carissa had almost forgotten that the nature faerie was currently perched on Raven's shoulder. Chaos smiled, especially after hearing she was missed. That was some gratitude, abandoning Carissa at the first sign of her old friend.

The captain spoke with the man in the black outfit, who pointed to the woman. The captain nodded. Carissa noticed but was too focused on the blow-up between the sisters to pay too much attention to anything else.

"Visiting friends is one thing, but playing with lives is dangerous, *Raven*."

"Perhaps we should talk in private," the captain finally spoke in an accent much like the man in black.

"Talk? With a murder to investigate?" Raven asked.

"The guards are more than capable," Macara said.

The captain instructed one of the elves to lead the two Tuatha de Danann women away. Neither woman acknowledged Cameron, Carissa, or Maren. Chaos waved. At least she remembered Carissa that much.

Cam cleared his throat, before they could leave, "Sir, as acting mayor of Moss Hill, I'd like to offer my assistance with what's happened here."

The captain turned around and took a moment to think about it.

"Sir, may I also be of assistance?" Varick asked.

The captain looked at the rank on Varick's nameplate. The bronze labeled him as a captain in his own right. Carissa wasn't sure if that ranked as highly as a ship captain of the royal fleet. It probably didn't, based on the way the ship captain addressed, not Varick, but the man in the black clothes.

"Warren, the king wishes us to be open with Moss Hill. Please share your findings with them."

"Is it a murder?" Carissa asked.

The captain raised an eyebrow. He glanced between her and Maren.

"Oh, um, we're with them," Carissa said.

Maren added, "She's Carissa Shae, she's also the—ow!"

Carissa lightly jabbed an elbow into Maren's side. This not-so-subtly stopped her from her embarrassing *do you know who she is* tirade. The captain answered.

"It appears to be an accident."

"Wasn't Raven just saying—" Cameron began.

Macara interrupted. "Cameron, Carissa, I'll explain everything later. Captain Heurle, if you would accompany us."

"Chaos, go tell the druidess to join us in Vale," Raven added.

Chaos lifted off Raven's shoulder and saluted. She zipped through the air in a flash. If they were calling for Jane, something more had to be going on. Carissa could not stand around and do nothing.

"What about the woman?" Carissa asked.

Macara and Raven were already walking away. If they heard her, they made no sign of it. The captain, however, did.

"Warren will answer your questions. Please excuse me," Captain Heurle replied.

He clicked his heels and bowed, then turned and walked away. Carissa, Maren, and Cam responded in kind. Maren, who wasn't used to curtseying, seemed to do something more like a parody of the gesture than the real thing.

"Curt, aren't they?" Maren asked as she rose.

Carissa shushed her with a headshake. It was odd, she had to admit, for them to be so secretive. Yet, from the little she knew of the Tuatha de Danann, the powerful fae ancestors never did anything without reason.

So what were Raven's reasons for coming to Moss Hill?

As they gathered around the guards and the body, a more pressing question arose: If this was an accident, what had Raven meant by saying they had a murder to solve?

Chapter 3

Dead in the Water

On the floor lay the woman in the green dress. Her arms were spread over her head like they had been flailing. A yellowish glow emanated from the hands of one of the guards. It reflected in the sheen of the boat floor. He knelt and methodically cast his magic over her from head to toe.

"I can detect changeling magic only," he announced when he was done.

Recognition sparked Carissa's elf-light. It tingled all through her body. Changelings had nearly taken over the entire town of Moss Hill a few months ago. Was this a changeling woman or one of her victims?

The rest of the guards reported. There were two types of magic on sight: changeling magic and that of a hazel wand. This seemed to appease the man in black clothes—Warren, the captain had called him.

Warren waved for the guards to remove the woman. Two of them knelt on either side of her and held their palms out toward each other. Strings of golden magic wove together under the woman, creating a stretcher of sorts.

As the four guards lifted her, Carissa saw a small, gray object fall from the woman's right hand. It was so light the wind carried it and so thin it fluttered through the air. If the guards had seen it, they must have dismissed it as a moth. No one made any attempt to grab it as it blew over the side of the boat.

"Who was she?" Cameron asked.

Warren hesitated before answering. Given the fact that the woman's body was still being carried away, Carissa could understand a somber tone, but Warren's came out harsh.

"This is Tamsin O'Mally," he said.

Maren gasped loud enough to grab everyone's attention. "Cari, *Tamsin O'Mally*, that was the troll woman Reg wrote about!"

Carissa didn't need reminding. Her racing mind put a stop to her mouth. Maren was right about it being the changeling troll woman whom Reg had said had snuck onto the king's boat in December. He never specified what her intentions were, but Carissa imagined it had something to do with the recent invasion of changelings trying to impersonate Mossies like Cameron. Carissa hadn't been aware that they were transporting her back to Moss Hill.

Varick seemed more interested in Warren than O'Mally.

"Forgive my asking: You are human, yet you are on the king's vessel?" Varick asked.

"I am a druid. Warren Skye." He introduced himself without offering a hand.

"Of the Hebrides islands?" Varick's eyes narrowed and he studied the man as intently as one would study an old book.

"I see my family reputation precedes me."

"It does," Varick said in a less than friendly tone. Warren didn't seem to care. Carissa made a mental note to ask him about this exchange later.

Cam looked between them before venturing to ask, "So, you were telling us about Mrs. O'Mally?"

"The sky darkened just as we were fetching the prisoner. She must've taken that as a chance to escape. My soldiers and I only caught up with her after she'd fallen from the stairway," Warren explained.

Carissa looked to the corridor where Macara and Raven had left. The sky darkening was definitely Raven. Her grand entrance may have led to this accident. Or had it been an accident? Raven herself had called it murder. But was she, at least in part, responsible?

"Did she attack or simply run?" Varick asked.

"She must've run. We found the cell empty."

"Did she fall down those stairs?" Maren pointed.

Varick's eyes didn't flicker with gold specs of magic ire the way they had when Carissa had first met him, but annoyance was visible. He was asking the questions. Maren took the hint and slumped.

Warren pointed upward. "I saw movement on the upper deck. She must've slipped from the railing before we reached the stairway, so we did not see whether she was hit."

That explained the hazel wand. Druidic magic required its use or that of something similar. Would Raven count that as murder? Carissa thought it only necessary to try to catch a prisoner.

"None of the guards saw it?" Cameron asked.

Varick flashed Carissa a can't-you-control-your-friends look. Carissa only pulled her lips to the side in a half-frown as if to say *just move on*. Varick showed great restraint limiting his annoyance to a scowl.

"Where is the ranking guard?" he asked.

"I *am* the ranking guard." Warren crossed his arms and puffed up his chest.

Varick's eyebrows raised. "I was not aware that any Warren was a member of the royal guard."

"I have been in service to the king for seven years."

The two locked eyes. Carissa and Maren exchanged an *enough with the machoism* eye roll. Cameron uttered a syllable, no doubt intending to quell the hostility, but a cheerful voice interrupted.

"Maren!"

The five of them turned to see the disheveled, reddish brown hair, glasses, and goofy smile of Reginald Smith heading toward them.

"Reg!" Maren laughed as he pulled her in for an embrace. "What are you wearing?"

Maren's boyfriend released her from a bear hug and scanned his long orange robe with his bespectacled eyes. His hands touched the gold buttons running down the chest.

"Do you like it? It's all the fashion in Tir-Na-Nog."

"It's, uh, nice." Maren's unconvincing tone was lost on Reg.

He beamed, but the heaviness of the situation still hung in the air. Toning down his good mood, Reg looked at Warren.

"I heard there was an accident?"

Instead of answering, Warren bowed. "If you'll excuse me, I have another prisoner to attend to."

Varick returned the gesture, but his eyes followed every footfall as the druid walked away. Carissa found herself doing the same. Maren wondered aloud about the druid.

"He didn't want to answer many questions, did he?"

"He's like that—not a man of many words." Reg explained. "Carissa, Cameron, how are you two?"

He pulled Cameron into a hug before he could say anything. Cam smiled awkwardly and patted Reg's back. Not noticing the expression, Reg hugged Carissa, too.

"Of course, Maren told me about the changelings and how brilliantly you handled that, Carissa."

Carissa acknowledged Reg's words with an embarrassed smile. Fortunately, Reg kept changing topic like a record on skip. Was he nervous or just excited to see them? It was probably both given Reg's curious personality.

He turned to Cameron again. "I hear you're the acting mayor, congratulations! Have they made that permanent yet?"

"Uh, no, the election is not for two more weeks."

"Cam was just giving a wonderful speech before you arrived," Maren explained.

Cam put a hand to the back of his neck. "Yeah, I'll have to reschedule it now."

Carissa rested a hand on Cameron's arm. Hours of rehearsing his speech, with Carissa in the role of the audience, had amounted to nothing. Which reminded her that the king's ship was not due in Moss Hill yet.

"Reg, we're glad to see you, but why did you arrive in Vale earlier than expected?" Carissa asked.

"Earlier? I guess we did. I don't know...good weather, I guess? Actually, the voyage went well, until, you know, the end."

"Did you see what happened?" Carissa asked.

"No, my room is on the other side of the ship. I thought I heard something as I was waking, but it must've been the storm."

While Reg asked Maren about her day's plans, movement in the water caught Carissa's attention. She made her way to the railing. The tarp lay on top of the water, half caught on a deck boat. She squinted. On top of the green backdrop, threatening to sink if not for the tarp, was a small triangular paper. Why would O'Mally have had a paper in her hands? Warren and his guards may have missed a vital clue.

Varick approached. Carissa expected him to growl an order at her to keep away from the crime scene. Instead, he stood next to her and looked where she was looking.

"What is it?"

Carissa leaned over the railing. There was nothing but blue water. Maybe the wind had carried the object farther away?

"What's going on?" Cameron asked.

He and the others had come closer. Maren bent over the railing, looking between the water and Carissa. Reg joined her a second later.

"What are we looking at?"

Carissa pointed. "There. O'Mally was holding that scrap of paper, but the wind blew it over the railing."

"I'll send a group to retrieve it."

"Wait," Carissa pleaded.

Only recently had she learned that her grandfather had been a Tuatha de Danann like Raven. Perhaps not exactly like Raven, or at least Carissa hoped not now that she'd seen her strange behavior. Either way, Carissa had inherited some of those powers and, thanks to the books in her grandfather's study, and to a certain nature faerie, she was learning to use them. The sprite had been around a Tuatha de Danann for a long time, so she knew a thing or two about their magic.

If what she taught her was right, Carissa could reach a hand over the water and will the paper into her hands. Closing her eyes and holding her palm downward, she focused on the object. After a few seconds of concentrating, Carissa felt something tickling her hand. It was thin and wet.

Please don't be a jellyfish. Turning her hand over, she found the scrap of triangular paper. Though soaked, it had a legible number on it: 10. Carissa showed it to the group.

"A number for a drawing?" Maren asked.

"Perhaps a message of some kind," Varick replied.

"The corner of a book page!" Reg blurted.

Cam took the paper from Carissa and turned it in his hand. "I think Reg is right."

"What book do you think it's from?" Maren asked.

"More importantly, why would Mrs. O'Mally be clutching a book page right before she died?" Carissa asked.

"The real question is: Why didn't the guards see it?" Cameron asked.

Varick smirked. "Elf guards. They're not as perceptive as the sidhe. It's no wonder they missed it."

Carissa bit her tongue. She could have reminded him of a time or two when the sidhe had fallen short of their duties. Even he wasn't perfect.

Finally, she had to ask, "Why did you let Warren go? You never got a full statement from him."

"He outranks me."

"Is he really part of the king's guard? He wasn't wearing the uniform," Maren said.

Reg chimed in, "He works freelance, if that's the right term, but he's been with the royals for years now. King Finvarra appointed Warren himself to be in charge of the prisoner and ship security for this mission."

"Why this mission?" Cameron asked.

"His specialty is catching changelings. Finvarra suspected a changeling in Tir-Na-Nog. Warren caught Tamsin O'Mally the first day he'd arrived on the island."

Carissa exchanged a look with Varick. Was it a coincidence that Warren had caught O'Mally so easily and that he'd been there upon her death? Carissa shook off the question. It was probably Varick's strange attitude that was making her question Warren. She wanted to ask Varick about his behavior toward the druid but thought it might not be best to ask it on the ship.

"We should probably go," Cameron said.

Varick held out his hand. "I'll take the paper. Perhaps my guards can determine its origin."

"Actually, would you mind if I did it?" Reg asked. "I'm at libraries all the time anyway. Besides, it's definitely not from any sidhe scrolls."

Carissa looked between Varick and Reg. She'd have kept the paper herself, but she had to admit that

Reg might be the most likely one to find the book to which it belonged. Slowly, she handed it to him. Varick did not argue.

As they all left, Maren said, "It was awful, Reg. O'Mally fell from the stairs."

"I know she was a changeling, but that's terrible! Was it...Did the guards...?" Reg couldn't quite finish the question.

Maren took Reg's arm as he helped her down the ramp. "It was an accident."

"If what Warren says is true," Varick muttered.

"What do you mean?" Reg asked.

"I think we should take Raven's advice and not rule out foul play," Carissa jumped in.

"I agree," Cameron said.

"I'm confused." Reg looked at Maren. "Didn't you say she fell?"

"That's what Warren said," Maren replied.
"But Raven called it murder," Carissa pressed, "and something tells me we ought to believe her."

Chapter 4

Reporter Rapport

Cameras flashed. Carissa blinked and shielded her eyes. The whole brigade of Moss Hill reporters awaited the ship's passengers. Cameron helped Carissa off the gangplank and was bombarded by microphones inches from his face. Carissa was brushed aside as reporters threw questions at him.

"Is there a reason for the boat's early arrival?"

"Why haven't the passengers disembarked yet?"

"Is it true there's been a murder?"

The last question came from behind the group, where some Mossies and, presumably, tourists watched in curiosity. It was asked by a woman in blue dress pants, a yellow blouse, and large sunglasses. She looked ready for TV with her blonde hair in a perfect bun resting atop her pretty face. Her figure was thin and her skin pale. The makeup gave her face a porcelain complexion, especially from a distance.

Cameron put a hand up, silencing the reporters. Handling the mayoral role with grace, he began, "The situation is perfectly under control. A passenger accidentally fell from an upper deck. Though tragic, there is no sign of foul play at this time."

"What about the mysterious woman who interrupted your campaign? Is she involved in this 'accident,'" the woman asked.

Varick met Carissa's eye and gave the slightest headshake. Cameron should not say anything about Raven. She agreed. In a public place like the marina, anyone could be around. Besides, this woman did not look like a Mossie, at least not one Carissa recognized.

"Involved? No," Cameron began.

Placing a hand on Cameron's back, Carissa gently tugged the fabric. Cameron got the hint. He stiffened and changed his tone.

"Uh, which news outlet are you with, Miss—what was your name?" Cameron asked.

"Jones. Morgan Jones of the *Cryptic Cipher Chronicles*."

Reg whispered, "That's a London paper."

"A London paper?" Cameron repeated.

The microphones picked this up. A few of the news reporters had turned toward the woman, scribbling notes as she spoke. Tilly, in particular, flashed a picture of her. Carissa could see the suspicion in Tilly's eyes. *Did she have the same unnerving feeling that this woman was close to divulging Moss Hill's secret?*

"Your strange town is gaining some attention, Mr. Larke. I'd say more so after today. Who was the mysterious woman making the magical entrance?"

"Magical?" Cameron's voice shook. "Oh, no, no, that was not magic. It was just theatrics. That is to say it *looked* like magic, but—"

"But what?" she demanded.

A voice interrupted from the crowd. "But it was just a prank to make the campaign more exciting."

Carissa could hear Cameron breathe a sigh of relief. Thankfully, a Mossie had stepped in to help keep the town's secrets. The only problem was the voice sounded all too familiar.

Carissa scrunched between Cameron and Maren, who leaned in to catch a view of the speaker. The Mossies parted, allowing the owner of the voice to step forward.

Carissa grasped Cameron's suit jacket tighter. Him? Wasn't he in jail? She let go as Cameron turned around. Both he and Carissa glared at Varick.

"Belkin is free?" Cameron asked.

Varick appeared unphased by the accusation-style question.

"He was not guilty of any crime."

"He lied to everyone!" Carissa said.

"He's a troll who tricked us into thinking he was human so that he could be mayor," Maren said—too loudly.

Carissa shushed her. Thankfully, the reporter seemed not to overhear.

Varick crossed his arms and whispered, "Humans lie all the time. And trolls are no longer banned from the island. There was no sentence to issue."

"Who are you?" Ms. Jones asked.

Belkin answered in his mayoral voice, full of authority. There was something else, too—a carefree composure. He strolled to join them at the base of the gangplank.

"Sean Belkin, former mayor of Moss Hill. And I assure you, Ms. Jones, that we are a strong community of diverse people. We love a good show and a fine bit of gossip. But, strange? I don't think that's the issue. I think it's more that we're strangers to you."

"So you wouldn't mind telling me more about the rumor about faeries inhabiting this island?"

A burst of laughter followed, first from the former mayor, then a nervous chuckling from the townsfolk. A few exclamations of "hogwash" and "foolishness" rose over the crowd. Belkin himself shook his head.

"What an imagination," he said as he turned his back to her.

Belkin made his way to the boat. Whispers overtook the crowd until he came face to face with Cameron. Belkin offered a hand.

"Congratulation on your campaign, my boy."

Cameron's eyes darted between Belkin's face and his outstretched hand. The old mayor smiled.

"I thought it would be a good idea for the two mayoral candidates to shake hands and wish each other well, don't you think?"

Carissa stood beside Cameron, whose eyes had widened considerably. He studied Belkin for a long time before taking the hand offered. It would not look gracious for him to reject the former mayor's handshake.

If the sound of the cheers once they locked palms was any indication, it seemed that Belkin may have a fair share of supporters in Moss Hill yet. Carissa looked out at the crowd. She had to admit that Belkin had deflected the reporter with some skill.

Ms. Jones might have been the only one in the crowd not smiling.

Belkin may have stopped her for the moment, but if the fae were not careful, reporters like her would almost certainly discover their existence. Especially if Raven Corvus kept up her shenanigans. Macara seemed to have her on good behavior as she clattered down the ramp.

Although perfectly able to walk of her own accord, Raven reached for Varick's arm as she stepped onto land. He offered her an elbow, which she took graciously as she waved to the crowd like royalty. Macara looked less than pleased. The captain, Warren, and three elf guards followed.

Raven asked Varick if he and his men would see them to Vale. To Cameron, she said, "I'm told I should apologize to you. Don't worry. I've promised my sister I wouldn't use any more 'theatrics,' as you called it." She winked at Carissa. "You've done well with the little chaos I've sent your way. We'll see each other again soon, Carissa."

Then Raven took a step and paused. Her eyes scanned Belkin up and down.

"For goodness sake, we're supposed to be hiding our true natures. Disguise yourself, sir."

"He *is* in disguise," Macara corrected her sister.

"Oh?" Raven tilted her head and studied him again. "I don't see it. Well, never mind. Let's go, I'm eager to meet the druidess." She looked at Varick. "Is your heart beating faster? That's an odd reaction. What's wrong?"

Varick stiffened. He signaled a command to one of his men. The sidhe guards ordered the crowd to disperse.

"Ma'am," Varick nudged.

Raven walked forward, setting the pace for the whole group. It was like a small battalion marching toward home. Mossies watched with awe.

"Was that Raven Corvus? Wait, ma'am!" Reg walked hastily behind the fae woman.

Carissa only hoped he didn't say the wrong thing in front of the reporter or any tourists.

"You'd better go with him," she said to Maren.

"I'm on it. See you later!" Maren called back.

Mayor Belkin chuckled. "Spirited friends, but spirit alone won't win Moss Hill. Good luck to you, Cameron. You're going to need it to have any chance against me."

Then, Belkin looked up at the ship. As the former mayor stepped back into the crowd, talking with some Mossies, Carissa turned her head to where he had been looking. There was no one there. What had he seen? Or was it possible he was waiting for someone?

Carissa waited for Cameron to finish telling the Mossies that today's events were over. He would hold another event in a few days' time. This was enough to persuade several of them to leave. At least the reporters had gotten the hint that he was no longer answering questions. By then, Carissa's parents walked down the gangway. They were led by two elf guards who were holding their luggage.

"Cari!" her mother exclaimed.

Once she'd made her way to solid ground, she hugged Carissa tightly. Her father directed the elf guards to take their luggage to their cottage in Vale. Then, he, too, embraced his daughter.

"Cari, we heard about the changeling invasion and we're glad you're all right," her father said.

"We're very proud of you," her mother added.

Carissa's cheeks reddened and she uttered a "thanks."

"Kaley, Dorian, it's good to see you both," Cameron greeted.

Carissa's father shook his hand. "Do we call you Mayor Larke now?"

"Or son-in-law, maybe?" her mother added.

Carissa's eyes flared. Her mother's smile only widened.

"Um, no, sir, I haven't been elected yet. We'll find out at the end of the month."

Carissa's father nodded. He patted Cameron's back and began walking. Carissa and her mother followed.

"Who's running against you?" her father asked.

"I was the first to announce."

"He was just launching his campaign today," Carissa said.

"Apparently, Belkin is running again," Cam mentioned.

After a moment of silence, her father said, "Perhaps it's best that Belkin remain in the position."

Carissa couldn't believe what she was hearing. "Dad, you can't be serious."

He put a gentle hand up. "I'm only looking out for his best interest. The position is a dangerous one."

"Dangerous?" Cameron asked. "You mean because Parker targeted Belkin?"

"That was a simple case of jealousy," Carissa reminded.

"That's not the only threat, as I think you know," her father retorted.

"The unseelie?" Cameron asked.

Carissa felt the slow, thudding pulse of her heart beat. No, she wasn't going to get anxious about the malevolent fae who hated everything Moss Hill represented. But Raven was here for a reason, she had warned Carissa for a reason, and perhaps her parents were dissuading Cameron from his mayoral run for a reason, too.

"Dad, is there something you know that you're not saying?"

"No, nothing specifically."

"Then don't you think Cameron would make a better mayor than Belkin?"

"I wouldn't brush off his years in office simply because he wasn't what you believed."

Carissa opened her mouth for another round of arguments, but her mother interrupted.

"Why don't we have some lunch?"

"We're headed to Carissa's right now," Cameron said.

He was seemingly upset by her father's statements, though he was doing his best not to show it. Carissa took his hand and squeezed as they continued toward the car.

"We're having the Larkes over for lunch," she said when they reached the car doors. *And if you say anything unsupportive of Cam, I will flip,* she wanted to add.

She was a bit touchy today.

Ever since Valentine's Day, the thought of his proposal kept entering her mind at every major event. Every Sunday at church, at the St. Patrick's Day celebrations, even one day when Cameron rented a sailboat for a daytrip around the island. Although, Maren invited herself to that one, which might have hindered the mood.

At first, Carissa had been convinced that she wasn't ready for marriage. But the moment he'd presented her with a beautiful ring that was not an engagement band, she had felt disappointed. She thought perhaps today....

"Perfect, we'll join you," Carissa's mother said...and the disappointment continued.

Carissa touched the Claddagh ring with her index finger. Friendship, loyalty, and love: his gift to her was beautiful. Even if it wasn't being used as an engagement ring, from the moment she'd started wearing it, life had been smooth sailing for Cameron and her. If only her parents could avoid rocking the boat.

Chapter 5

Family Gatherings

Cameron's parents hadn't wanted anything fancy. Just a simple outdoor lunch on a beautiful spring day. That meant potato salad and sandwiches. And, of course, a cherry cobbler, per Chaos's request, which Nan stuck in the oven while Carissa mulled over the many ways today was going wrong.

Closing the oven door, Nan said, "Sometimes, I think you are half-vampire rather than half-elf the way you bite that lip of yours."

Carissa looked up. Her nervous habit had a way of coming out at the worst times. She let her lip go.

"Sorry."

Nan smiled and moved on to the tossed salad. It was mostly prepared, except that Nan liked to add extra tomatoes. She did so, then tossed it a few more times with the tongs. All the while, she gave no outward notice that Carissa had stopped her potato salad preparations.

"You're really not going to ask me what's wrong?" Carissa asked.

"I don't have to."

"What? Why not?"

"You're nervous about your first lunch with Cameron's parents, and your parents are now joining us, so you're worried they'll just show the Larkes how *fae* you are and how different from a human."

Carissa's teeth found her bottom lip again. She couldn't help it. Nan had bluntly stated her fears. Only, she wasn't completely right.

"I've met Cam's parents before, several times. They know I'm part fae," Carissa explained.

"Yes, and you know how critical they are, but none of it mattered before because you weren't dating their son."

Carissa closed her eyes and sighed. "They've always liked me. I don't think their opinion of me will change."

"I'm sure it will."

Carissa's eyelids flew open. Nan laughed and grasped her chin lightly.

"They liked you before. Now, they'll come to love you."

Nan tasted the potato salad and gave Carissa an approval nod. Carissa grinned. The smile disappeared with the doorbell and suddenly vampiric Carissa was back. Nan swatted her shoulder.

"Stop chewing that lip and go join Cam and your parents. I'll get the door."

Carissa took a deep breath. *Here goes nothing.* She stepped through the sliding glass doors with the potato salad in one hand and sandwich platter in the other. Cam grabbed the sandwiches, probably equally from hunger and to be helpful. By the time they were set on the table under the aqua umbrella, Nan came out with Cameron's parents following behind.

Unlike Carissa's parents' warm hugs, Cameron's mother greeted him with a peck on the cheek and his father with a handshake. To Carissa and her parents, there was a friendly hello before they took their seats. Nothing more was to be expected.

"Everything looks delicious," Carissa's mother praised.

Carissa set it within easy reach of Cameron, knowing it was one of his favorites. He gave her a kiss as she sat on the white, wooden chair to his right. Dr. Reagan Larke reached one hand to his wife and one to his son as Carissa's mother reached for a sandwich. Both of the Larke's eyes opened wide.

"The Larkes always say grace before a meal," Carissa explained.

Her mother pulled her hand back into her lap.

"I hope you don't mind," Dr. Larke said.

"No, always good to show thanks. May I say the grace?"

"I don't think—" Carissa started.

"That would be lovely," Dana finished.

Carissa closed her eyes and put her head down, wanting to plunge her face into her palm.

"Dear God or Goddess, who may or may not exist, from whichever religion the people at this table believe in—I'm guessing Catholic like my daughter—bless this food or at any rate don't curse it. We thank you."

Carissa made a silent prayer of her own: that her mother would not say another word throughout the meal. Nan's wry under-the-breath chuckle and headshake led the way for a nervous laugh from Cameron.

"That was…interesting," Dana said.

"To say the least," Reagan added.

This earned him a sharp look from his wife. To break the tension, Carissa lifted the spoon for the potato salad and held a hand out for Reagan's plate. Even before she could say the words "would you like some" he held up a hand.

"No, thank you, I don't care much for potato salad."

Carissa frowned. Cameron hadn't mentioned that his father did not like the dish. His mother, however, held her plate out to Carissa.

"It's one of my favorites, thanks," she said.

Gratefully, Carissa's face brightened as she scooped a heaping spoonful onto the plate. Carissa heard the tinkling sound of faerie wings and hoped Hiya would not fly up onto the plate. Instead, a group of nature faeries gathered on the flowers around the sibling faeries. Hiya and Cynth stood on the top of the hyacinth flowers, excitedly telling them about all that had happened this morning—including the part about the ship's arrival. Based on what Carissa could make out, the naughty sprites had spied on the whole commotion. At least they hadn't been seen, or so she hoped.

"…Separation from Vale?"

Her father's voice interrupted her thoughts. She'd missed something. What was he bringing up now?

Whatever it was, Reagan replied, "We don't support separation from Vale, but it has been a long time since any of us could trace our lineage directly to the fae. We are human, so it's nice to have more contact with the outside world."

"Dad," Cameron began.

"No, no, please don't misunderstand. I'm just trying to share what many Mossies think. You have the Otherworld. You can travel anywhere in the Otherworld and connect with any other fae."

"Any Mossie can travel through the human realm the same way," her mother pointed out, "and don't tell me that any fae can come to Moss Hill because they can't."

"Why is that?" Carissa asked.

She genuinely had never discussed this with her parents. They had never taught her to use her powers. They were never home. And now, they were stating the obvious: Moss Hill was off limits to other fae.

"Slip of the tongue. I meant they don't. Moss Hill just isn't as exciting to the fae as other places in the world. Very few settled here and no one else has been interested."

"Except the unseelie," Carissa said.

Her father tilted his head. Translation: *Do not press the issue.* Her mother lowered her sandwich.

Dana said, "We may already have unseelie on the island. Even our previous mayor was a troll."

"To be fair, he isn't unseelie either," Nan said.

How like Nan to see the good in people. Carissa wanted her first thoughts about people to be like that, but her sentiments were more in line with Cameron's mother.

"A lie is a lie," Dana said. "And it seems like the lies and the *pretending to be human* is becoming more common lately."

Nan said, "Since we've opened the island to tourists. Yes, the unseelie took it as an opportunity, sadly."

"I'm in favor of the increase in tourism. No, that's not what worries me."

"Dad, please don't," Cameron begged.

But his father had already started. "I understand that we all have some fae blood and that Moss Hill started out with good intentions. That was a long time ago, though. We're not fae. Keeping your existence secret, well it's kept us away from our own kind."

"You think we've hurt you?" Carissa's father asked.

"No, that's not what he means," Dana reassured. "Please don't misunderstand us. We've, well, we just thought that maybe future generations of our family might move on from life on an island."

"Here we go." Cameron dabbed his lips with his napkin and set it down, seeming to have given up on his lunch.

"Charlie moved from Moss Hill last year and he's doing very well for himself," Dana said.

"I'm not Charlie," Cam said.

Charlie, Cameron's cousin, had recently completed his residency in London and moved there to be welcomed by a substantial salary and an apartment with a direct view of the Big Ben. Why the clocktower was a point of pride was beyond Carissa. She put a hand on Cameron's as his mother continued.

"Cam, we're not comparing you to anyone. We're very proud of you. And we like you, Carissa. But there's a whole world out there—we just want to make sure you're not missing anything. I'm sure *you* understand."

She looked at Carissa's mother and then at Nan. The implication was clear: *You're both human, so of course you understand how scary it is to have fae pretending to fit in with us.* If only she knew that the very human Nessa Shae had married not just any fae, but a Tuatha de Danann. Carissa herself hadn't known until recently that, while her father was a high-status elf, her mother had a lineage far more powerful than a regular faerie.

Nan might be thinking the same thing, considering the amused smile on her lips. Carissa's mother joined Cameron in setting her napkin on the table. She smiled and pushed her chair out. Her father did the same.

"Any parent wants whatever's best for their children—when it's possible. If you'll excuse us, we have to be getting back to Vale. Thank you, Mother, for the lunch."

"We have cherry cobbler for dessert," Nan offered, as unaffected as a person could seem in the midst of an argument.

"We'll pass, thanks. Carissa and Cameron, happy as ever to see you both well. Mr. and Mrs. Larke, lovely to meet you. Take care, everyone!"

With a handwave, she made a beeline for the screen door. Her father bowed in elf fashion and joined in his wife's hurried exit. Carissa excused herself and walked her parents out.

"There's no need to see us off, Cari," her mother said.

She ignored it. Once they were inside, she closed the patio behind them.

"I know the Larkes were a little—"

"It's not the Larkes." Her mother kept walking.

"Then what's going on?" Carissa threw up her hands.

"Nothing," her mother's voice was nonchalant as she made it to the front door.

"Dad?" Carissa touched his shoulder before he made it out of the house.

Her father placed a hand atop hers. "Why don't you come tonight and bring us some of the cobbler? We'll talk then," he said, gently squeezing her hand.

She was left puzzled by their departure. Had Mr. Larke offended them? She didn't need to think long about that one. She had to work hard not to feel offended herself. Then again, maybe humans did have a need for human companionship. Didn't she sometimes feel torn between Vale and Moss Hill? The fae could be…overwhelming. Sidhe propriety, elfish tempers, and even the intimidating demeanor of the Tuatha de Danann—all of it felt like too much sometimes. But humans had their nosiness, their quickness to blame, *their fear*, she realized.

She'd seen how frightening the fae world could be for Cameron. He was brave enough to stick with her through all the magic and mayhem, but would he want to forever? Even being mayor of Moss Hill had proven to be more difficult today than it might be in any other town—trying to calm the Mossies after Raven's arrival while hiding fae secrets from tourists who might reveal Moss Hill's true nature to the world.

And what if he wanted to travel? What if he wanted the apartment across from Big Ben in an interesting city with a mix of humans from all over the world? Cari loved Moss Hill. She was sure she'd never want to live anywhere else.

A thought occurred to her that never had before. What if her mother had loved Moss Hill just as much? *"Any parent wants whatever's best for their children—when it's possible."* That's what her mother had said. Why wouldn't it be possible? And was her mother talking about Carissa or herself? Could she have been misunderstanding her parents all these years?

Feeling her stomach churning, Carissa tried to push down her emotions and sit back next to Cameron as if nothing was wrong. The conversation seemed to have gone on as normal, with Nan chuckling at something Dana had said. Cameron absently placed his arm on her back and rubbed. The slightest look in her direction told Carissa that he not only was aware of her dismay, but that everything would be all right.

She couldn't help but turn thoughts over in her mind through the rest of the lunch. She tried to be jovial and polite. The Larkes kept to happier topics, too. And by the time the desserts had come, Dana made something of an apology.

"I hope we didn't offend you, Cari, or your parents. You know we respect you all."

Raegan said, "Oh, they know it. Don't you?"

Cameron leaned toward Carissa and said in a quiet voice they could all clearly hear, "My parents like you even better than they like me."

"Possibly better than Charlie, too." Raegan winked.

Carissa felt the tension in her throat relaxing. She could laugh without her chest hitching. The rest of the meal passed in peace. When Cameron's parents left and his arms wrapped around her as they waved goodbye to Dana and Raegan, she allowed herself to shake off the feelings she'd had at lunch. Her elf-light calmed around her heart. The warmth was a gentle reminder that of all the doubts that had arisen in her mind, the one question that had not was whether Cameron loved her.

***

THERE WAS NO one picking up the phone at the Seelie Tree Apothecary. Holly had learned to answer telephones, but maybe she was being finicky about using the technology. She had her stubborn streaks.

Since Cameron was needed at the mayor's office to assess the damage from Raven's arrival and to reschedule his campaign speech, Carissa thought she might as well go in and see for herself. Holly would be glad to have the afternoon off to see Macara. Had she known the boat would arrive early, Carissa would have given Holly the time off anyway. Besides, Carissa wasn't used to taking days off.

There was another reason for going in, too. Raven said she'd need the ankou to help solve the murder. Carissa knew why. If Mrs. O'Mally had died in Moss Hill, he was the one who would have retrieved her spirit. If that was the case, he could straight out ask her what had happened to cause her death.

Luckily, the Grim Reaper was a friend of Carissa's. The only problem was the ingredients for the spell to summon him were in the apothecary shop. It would have been easier to have Holly collect the necessary items—if only she would answer the phone. For that matter, Carissa wouldn't have needed the spell if Chaos hadn't abandoned her. The nature faerie could summon the ankou at will. Without her,

Carissa had no choice but to grab her blue beach cruiser bicycle and head to the shop.

The day was pleasant enough now that Raven was not traveling in any magically created tempests. The journey through her neighborhood—Crescent Circle, past the path Vale Mountain and to the right on Gorse Street—was at most twenty minutes. When she arrived, the shop's lights were not on. Carissa unlocked the door and looked up at the clock. At 2:10 p.m. lunch was over, and the shop should have re-opened for the afternoon.

"Holly?" Carissa called out. "Are you still eating lunch? It's getting late."

No one was in the back room. Could Holly be at the bakery next door? Or had she locked up the minute she'd heard Macara had returned to Moss Hill?

Guilt twisted her stomach. She should have called Holly right away. The leprechaun woman, or bean tighe as she referred to herself, might have been angry with her for letting two hours pass before letting her know the good news. Fae like Holly weren't used to jobs with set hours. Though Carissa had thought she knew better than to abandon the store like that.

Carissa sat in the office for a minute, feeling bad about Chaos abandoning her and Holly deserting the shop before deciding it wasn't right to sulk. She had an ankou to summon.

She found a small bag she kept locked in the bottom drawer of her desk and reread the instructions. Sparking the powder with her elf-light, she uttered, "Show thee, ankou," and waited. The hair on the back of her neck stood up. Alden always showed up behind her, in the other room, or ten minutes later, whichever was most unexpected. And he was always in spectral form when he did it. It was like he was trying to be scary. This time she was determined not to yelp.

She failed. The skeletal ankou's face appeared in the turned off monitor screen, eyes glowing like fire behind her. She took a moment to catch her breath before turning around. By now, Alden had shifted into his old human appearance.

"I never mean to scare you." His usual apologies took on a sadder tone each time.

"It's fine, really."

He looked at the bag on the computer desk. The summoning powder was not usually needed. She picked it up.

"Just needed this because Chaos is not with me at the moment."

"Is she okay?" he asked.

"Yes, she's just with an old friend. Raven Corvus came to Moss Hill this morning."

"Raven's here? That might be who I sensed."

"With the tornado she came in, I think all of Moss Hill sensed her," Carissa joked.

"She likes to make an entrance."

"You talk about her like you know her. Have you met Raven before?"

"Miss Morgan used to tell stories about her and Macara. Jane was always scared of 'the battle crow.'"

"Battle crow?"

"Everywhere she goes she brings a battle. It's not a good omen if she's in Moss Hill. It means danger is coming."

Carissa nodded. Technically, with the arrival of the nature faerie, Moss Hill had experienced plenty of danger. Raven had predicted it in her note. But, this statement made her wonder even more: Was there a connection between Raven's arrival and O'Mally's death? Had she predicted danger or caused it?

"A troll woman passed away on a ship in the marina this morning. Her name is Tamsin O'Mally."

Alden said, "There is a spirit, or something, wandering around Moss Hill. I didn't sense the actual death. Though, I should be able to sense it if it's anywhere near the island."

"It might've been a little out at sea. They weren't specific about the time."

"If it was on a ship, it's possible my ankou powers only work on land."

"So, who collects the souls if a person dies out at sea?"

He shook his head. "I don't know all the ankous in the world. There might be one specific to water. I'll take a look around the marina. If there's a wandering soul there, I'll find her."

"Raven said she was murdered."

Alden's head sank and his lips pinched together. All he had to do was put a hand on his chin and his face was Rodin's *The Thinker* statue.

"I thought you could find O'Mally's spirit and ask her what happened," Carissa prompted.

"I already followed her a little, I think."

"Where?"

"She's wandering all over Moss Hill. It's almost like she's lost."

"Or she's looking for her killer. I wonder if anything else has left the ship," Carissa said.

"Maybe," Alden said. This time he looked right at her. It was unnerving staring into an ankou's eyes.

They were blue with an endless black at the center. It was even more upsetting when he held a solemn, gripping gaze. "I know you like Chaos. I like her, too. But I wouldn't trust Raven, Carissa. Morgan and Macara both warned Jane and me about her. She doesn't just fight wars; she thrives off of them. I'd be careful around her."

She shuddered. Alden stepped back as if both surprised and sorry. She felt a little guilty for the reaction, but she genuinely felt a chill at his words.

"I'll be careful," she said, "I promise."

Chapter 6

Parting the Vale

Shrieks pierced the town of Vale. Banshees would be put to shame to hear them. The cry of a single sidhe soldier set them off.

"The prisoners have escaped!"

Then the cry of, "Humans! Humans loose in Vale."

Several fae, from brownies to trooping faeries, scrambled from their treelike cottages and earthen-sculpted homes and took to the streets with lamplight. A particularly loud screech caused Carissa to clutch her left ear while nearly dropping the cherry cobbler in her right hand. A gnome ran into her calf and spun her around. As she lifted her leg to cradle what was definitely going to become a bruise, she caught sight of Sal.

The elfkin servant of the head elf of Vale jumped over a pair of duergars on his way past the border into the fae town. His long legs stumbled and the bundle in his hands bounced. Clothes landed in a thump on the ground. Sal bent to pick them up, tripping a ghillie dhu in the process.

"Watch it." The short, black-haired man picked up his moss hat and continued on his way.

Carissa ran over to help Sal with the last of his items.

"Thanks, Cari." Sal took the clothing.

"Sal, why is everyone panicking?"

Sal rummaged through the laundry. "I haven't the slightest idea. I've been out washing these. I hope I won't have to wash them again."

As he adjusted them for easy carrying, he sniffed and looked that the pie. He didn't need to ask. Carissa opened the lid with a smile and a "help yourself."

"Oh no, I couldn't," he said, though his black eyes followed the container.

Carissa's eyes followed the villagers.

Snapping the pie lid shut, Carissa said, "Someone around has to know something. Sir?"

Sal pried his eyes away from the cherry cobbler and joined in. "Ma'am? Miss, if you could stop a moment."

They tried a few vain attempts to get anyone's attention. After three, Sal stopped and scratched his head. Dropping his hand, he shouted, "Watch out!" as another form nearly smacked into the two of them.

"Sorry, in a hurry." A tall tylwyth teg, whose green skin glowed in the moonlight, said.

Carissa gently caught her shoulder. "Wait, Tabitha, what's going on?"

"Carissa? Did the sidhe call you for help, too?"

"The sidhe don't call on people to help."

"They call on me. Well, I asked, but they accepted my help."

"With what? What's going on?"

"The humans who kidnapped Barnaby and Holly have escaped. Now there's humans wandering around in Vale. And not Mossies, these were *tourists*."

Carissa blinked several times. "Barnaby and Holly were kidnapped?"

Carissa felt sick. It explained why Holly hadn't been in the shop. She should have realized Holly wouldn't just discard her duties like that. She should have known something was wrong. But there had been no sign of struggle.

"Slow down and start at the beginning. And tell me everything," Carissa said.

"It was this afternoon. I went over to see them. I stopped by the bakery first."

Carissa realized her mistake. "Not everything, Tabitha, just tell me about the kidnapping itself."

"Right. They were taken by two humans who thought Barnaby could lead them to treasure."

"Treasure?" Sal asked.

Carissa put a hand to her forehead. "Leprechaun treasure. There's a silly human legend that leprechauns have pots of gold at the end of rainbows."

"I didn't know leprechauns did that," Sal said.

"They don't. At least, I know Barnaby doesn't."

"Good thing the kidnappers didn't know that, though, because Holly took them all the way to the creek by my home where I found and rescued them."

Tabitha's skin took on a lighter green shade that Carissa interpreted as pride. She didn't point out the fact that if the kidnappers had known that leprechauns didn't keep treasure they probably wouldn't have taken the leprechauns. Instead, she breathed a sigh of relief.

"I'm so sorry I wasn't there to help. How are Barnaby and Holly? Were they hurt?"

"They're fine for now, but those people might try again. I have to go back and warn them."

Carissa put a hand out to stop Tabitha's mad dash to the nearest adder stone portal to Moss Hill. The portals didn't work for everyone, but changelings like Tabitha could use their particular brand of magic to travel through the large circular stones to wherever they were placed all over town. Once gone, she'd be out of reach in a flash.

Fortunately, Tabitha paused and turned around.

"Is that cherry cobbler?" she asked.

Carissa handed her the whole container to take to Barnaby and Holly. She also took the opportunity to ask her few last questions.

"How many humans were there?"

With how the fae were rushing about, it seemed like it should be a large number. But, Tabitha informed them that there were two.

"A big furry man and a woman—not bad looking—blonde, green-eyed, and pretty."

"Furry man? Are you sure he was human?" Carissa asked.

"I think she means hairy," Sal replied.

"They were human, at least I think so. They kept calling themselves tourists—that's a human thing, isn't it?"

Carissa slowly lowered her chin. They were supposed to be human anyway. With Cameron's parents' words replaying in her mind, she wondered about that now.

"Tabitha, could you go to Maren's first? She can call Barnaby and Holly and take you to the police station."

"The human police?"

"For human tourists," Sal said. "Makes sense to me."

Carissa guessed neither of them had heard about Cameron's initiative to improve communication between the police and sidhe guard. It had been slow-going, but the Sidhe Council had agreed. This would be a prime opportunity to see it in action.

Finally, Tabitha agreed, then waved goodbye and dashed off without another word. Sal started walking toward his master's home. His lanky form moved slowly enough for Carissa to follow, but fast enough to show he was nervous.

"I never would have thought we'd see humans in Vale—except the Mossies, of course. How would tourists even know Barnaby was a leprechaun?"

Carissa didn't answer. She could only think of one non-Mossie who'd recognized the fae folk on first sight. Reginald. But was he the only one who knew enough about the fae to identify them? Or was he just the first one they'd met?

She had spent so much time worrying about unseelie faeries in town that she hadn't even considered how many humans might come to Moss Hill for nefarious purposes. Maybe her mother, being part Tuatha de Danann, could help set up some defenses around Vale to make it harder for humans to get to. She shook her head. Now she was thinking like the Larkes.

Saying goodnight to Sal, she turned left down the lane to the cottage with the slow burning fire in the hearth. Smoke of changing colors puffed through the chimney. They were cooking something full of spice. The peppery scent tickled her nose.

Grabbing the door knocker, Carissa banged it three times in quick succession. Footsteps were followed by the creak of the opening door. Her father's friendly face welcomed her.

"Come in, love," her father said softly.

"I've lost the cobbler, sorry to say."

Her father did not acknowledge the statement. She'd expected at least a smile. Carissa stepped in the direction of the kitchen, then stopped. There was a pot of something boiling in the fireplace. Her father placed an open palm toward the living room chair.

"Please, sit down."

"Are you cooking something?"

Her mother came in with a mortar and pestle, though both were lit with amber-colored magic. Carissa looked back and forth between her parents, both of whom were more serious than she'd ever seen them before. She stepped back.

"A little faster, Cari. We haven't got all night."

"Kaley, shouldn't we give her a little context first."

"She's late and I've got it all prepared."

"We're scaring her. The magic will hold ten minutes. Carissa, could you please sit down?"

"Oh, all right." Her mother dropped the brush into the bowl and sank into the sofa cushions. Her father took the chair opposite the one he'd pointed to earlier.

"What's going on?" Carissa asked.

"Something we should have done a long time ago," her father said.

"Now you're explaining backwards, Dorian. You sound positively threatening. Sit, Carissa. *I'll* explain."

Carissa approached the chair like it was her execution. She trusted her parents, but they'd never acted this strangely. She flashed back to the changelings a month ago, who'd kidnapped and taken the place of other townsfolk. Studying her parents' moves, she thought of questions she could ask to make sure they were really themselves.

Before she could lay eyes on her mother, Kaley Shae proved her half-Tuatha de Danann status by reaching toward the fireplace and taking a small flame. It leapt from the fire and danced on her hand. Then it faded in a puff of smoke and her mother waved her hand with an "ouch." Carissa sat, dumbfounded.

"That's the trick Macara did for you, isn't it?"

Carissa nodded. It had been more impressive with Macara, but it was essentially the same.

"There, then I've shown you I'm Tuatha de Danann, in part anyway. Let's see, what else? Your favorite place is your garden at Nan's. When you're here, you like to sit on the boulder in our backyard and you met your favorite nature faeries, Hiya and Cynth, when Hiya fell into our fountain. Is that enough or should I keep going?"

"Enough for what? Why are you telling me this?"

"Because you were thinking 'they're acting strangely, I wonder if they're changelings in disguise.'"

"Is that another power of the Tuatha de Danann, reading minds?"

"No, it's the power of a mother. I know my own daughter."

Carissa could have argued that her mother was never around enough to know her daughter that well, but she held her tongue. Carissa had never told her parents how she'd felt about their constant traveling. Since she was the real Kaley Shae, she would only be hurt by the revelation. Besides, Carissa was a grown woman with a business and a boyfriend of her own. She couldn't still be hurt about their absence now.

Her father took the mortar from her mother. It glinted gold in the light of the crackling fire. It almost looked like MacLir's Cup of Truth.

"Carissa, your mother and I have always wanted what's best for you. That's why we decided not to teach you to use your powers."

Finally, here was a chance for Carissa to confront them.

"Did you think I would misuse the power? Or that I wouldn't be able to master it?"

"Your power was locked, and not by me," her mother explained.

"Not your elf-light, just your Tuatha de Danann powers were withheld from you," her father clarified.

"Who locked them?"

"Your grandmother told me you unlocked the study?" her mother asked.

"In February. We needed an adder stone."

"You'll need a lot more of what's in that study in the future."

"And you'll need this."

Her father took the pot off the fire and poured it into the mortar. It steamed. Her mother took the pestle and ground whatever was in the bowl. Then she handed it to Carissa.

"Dried herbs? Wasn't it liquid just a moment ago?"

"The liquid was the magic. It has infused itself into the herbs," her father explained.

"Give me your necklace," her mother said.

"My locket?" Carissa's fingers touched the circular glass with herbs set in the middle. Her mother had given it to her when she was a child. It allowed her to see into the Otherworld and human world at the same time. She rarely took it off.

Slowly, Carissa lifted it over her head. Her mother opened the locket and dumped the herbs into the fireplace. They sparked with puffs of bright white light.

Inside the empty locket, she placed the new herbs and said an incantation. Then she sealed the locket once again. Carissa did not feel any different, but the herbs glowed bright orange and faded to normal.

"What is this?"

"It's not just an Otherworld locket," her father said.

"It's a talisman," her mother finished. "It has protected you from detection, but the spell was made with my magic alone."

"This was made with Macara's and MacLir's magic. It should protect you in this world, the Otherworld, and the Afterworld," her father explained.

"The Afterworld?"

"Where the ankou resides."

"She won't need to go there," her mother interrupted. "It's just a precaution MacLir insisted on."

"Why are you giving me this?"

"Because…" her mother started and stopped.

"Macara will explain tomorrow."

"Why tomorrow? Why not tonight?"

"Macara and Raven are speaking with Sidhe Council. They'll have a lot to discuss," her father said.

"You mean argue over," her mother corrected.

"Macara will explain tomorrow after our return party."

"Everyone is invited to our home for an early dinner. Invite Reginald, Maren, Barnaby, the more the merrier," her mother said.

"Once the party is over, we'll be able to speak freely."

"Now go. And be careful out there."

Carissa's mother ushered her to the door. Her father added that she ought to get home before it was fully dark outside. She nearly laughed as she opened the door.

"Because of the humans loose in Vale? I can handle a few tourists."

"Not a tourist, your mother sensed something else at the house."

Carissa closed the door as quickly as she opened it. Turning around, she asked, "What did you sense?"

"Something from the Afterworld," her mother said.

"An ankou? You know I'm friends with Alden."

"Maybe not an ankou. I don't know. But I will tell you this, even if it was Alden standing in the shadows of the house, that is not a good sign. Ankous never go anywhere without a reason."

"Go, get home safely," her father said.

Carissa reluctantly agreed. So many things about this day were strange. She wondered what else could happen in the few short hours that were left. Pulling the door shut and stepping onto the now deserted street, she felt a chill run down her spine. It wasn't just the eerie stillness of the outside. She felt someone was watching her.

The tree beside her rustled.

"Who's there?" she asked, thankful that she was still close enough to the house to run back inside.

The tree branch wobbled as if something had launched off of it. Carissa put her arms up to defend herself. A chiming sound filled the air and whatever had come out of the tree was zooming toward her head. The blurred figure came into focus. A three-inch nature faerie hovered inches from her face.

"Chaos! There you are, finally decided to come back?"

Chaos nodded, snuggling into her hair like it was a blanket and curling into a ball. She smiled. The sprite may have abandoned her during the day, but she did return home before the day was out. And now she wouldn't have to walk alone. Though, there might be one more person who could walk her back safely to Moss Hill.

"Before you sleep, could you please call on Alden?" Carissa asked.

Chaos rubbed her eyes. Then, putting out her hand like it was a chore, she waved it. Faerie dust flew.

Carissa waited.

"Nothing's happening, Chaos. Chaos?"

A light wind chime began whistling in her right ear, signaling to Carissa that the nature faerie had fallen asleep. Carissa scooped Chaos into her palm and continued walking.

A sudden chill filled the air and a gust of wind played through her hair where Chaos had just been resting. Carissa turned. The grim sight of the skeletal ankou morphed before her eyes into the presence of an old friend.

"Alden," Carissa said.

She might just have to accept that she would always be startled by the ankou. Even when she was expecting him, he was an unnerving friend to have. She did try to hide her startled wince as a smile.

"Did you find anything?" she asked.

Alden walked with her as she resumed the journey to Moss Hill, answering, "I don't sense a recently departed spirit in Moss Hill."

"She's hiding?"

"No, I'd be able to detect a spirit."

"You weren't aware your grandfather was still in Moss Hill. Is it possible you've just missed her?"

Alden shook his head. "My grandfather wasn't a spirit. He was the previous ankou. There's a difference. And, honestly, I didn't sense him because I didn't realize that I'd been feeling his presence all along."

"What does that mean?"

"He was ankou before me, which means he was still around from the moment I became ankou. I was new to the experience, so I didn't realize that I was sensing him."

"So, you can sense spirits and ankous? How does that help us?"

"Well, I know I'm not sensing a spirit, but I also know I am sensing something."

"Another ankou?"

"I can't tell yet. Ankou powers grow the longer they've been connected to the world beyond. It could be a new ankou, just starting out, or…"

"Or?"

"A very old ankou who has learned to mask their powers."

Carissa blinked several times, no longer concentrating on the path ahead. Her walking slowed until her thoughts caught up with her. She paused.

"You think Mrs. O'Mally is becoming a new ankou?"

"I'm not sure that it's her. I'm not sure what it is."

"Can you track it?"

"I've been trying, but the sensations aren't clear. I've ended up all over the place today trying to track whoever, or whatever, this is."

"Where has it taken you?"

"The marina, the woods, my parents' home, even…"

He looked down. His eyes avoided her. Her tilted her head curiously.

"Where?" she asked.

"Your home."

Realization struck. "That's what my mother sensed. She said we were being watched."

"You probably were. But it wasn't just by me."

"Why would Mrs. O'Mally be in all those places?"

"Carissa," Alden quickened his pace and stepped in front of her, "I *really* don't think it's Mrs. O'Mally. Someone, *something*, is watching you. And it's not an ordinary fae."

His words stayed with her right up to the front porch of her home. Once inside, she settled Chaos on a doily on her dresser and walked over to her grandfather's study. Quietly, so as not to wake anyone, she placed her hand on the door and allowed her Tuatha de Danann magic to do its work.

A sleepy nature faerie joined her within a moment. She would have told Chaos to go back to bed, but she was grateful to the sprite for being there. Chaos looked up at her with half-closed eyes and a raised brow. Carissa answered the wordless question.

"I've got to find out more about the Afterworld." *Especially if something is after me*, she thought.

Chapter 7

Easter Eggs

The hunt was near. Soon after Sunday service, the peaceful churchyard filled with the frenzy of the chase. The Easter eggs stood no chance.

Father Quinn blew the whistle and the annual children's Easter Egg Hunt began with squeals of delight from fae and human children alike. There were even a few nature faeries in the mix helping the children find their eggs—including Chaos, Hiya, and Cynth. They were adorable in their new spring clothes and flower hats. Hiya looked sporty in his blue rosebud cap, though he'd probably lose it by the end of the day as he was roughly darting in and out of bushes. Cynth lagged behind while fussing with her pink carnation bonnet. Chaos threw hers off immediately to beat Hiya to the eggs.

All the churchgoers with young ones attended to them, and all those without hosted the lemonade stands, the dessert tables, or any of the little things that added up to the perfect event. Carissa worked first aid today. She offered Band-Aids, sunscreen, umbrellas, and blankets for those who wished to lay out a picnic. There were only a few incidents that required her attention throughout the morning.

Little Alayna, Carissa's neighbor, Anne's child who was just learning to walk, fell in the grass and scraped her knee. Carissa cleansed it with a lavender wash and put a Band-Aid over it. Mr. Greer's great-nephews switched baskets to play a trick on an elf child and came away with a magic-induced burn. Carissa treated it with medicinal honey on a gauze and left the reprimanding to the child's mother.

By noon, the hunt had settled down, and Mrs. Larke relieved Carissa of her first aid duties. This left Carissa free to wander over to Cameron as he passed out campaign buttons. She took a few and passed them out herself.

"Mrs. Alcott, does Cameron have your vote in this election?"

Mrs. Alcott did not take the button.

"You know I want to support Cameron, Carissa, but I'm not anything if not fair. So, I can't say yet who I'll be voting for until I hear their debate next Saturday."

Mrs. Harbridge interrupted as she pinned a button on her own yellow dress. "Rosa, you know you're going to vote for Cam. Mr. Belkin was a troll, for goodness sake, and I'm not even using hyperbole. Heaven knows I wish I was."

"Trolls, brownies, leprechauns...that's what Moss Hill is about, Patsy. I can't discount anyone until I've heard them both out. Fair is fair."

"Fine. Cameron? Dear, tell her what you were telling me about the ferry boat."

Carissa's eyes widened. Had he told her about the suspected murder on the ferry? Mrs. Harbridge would have the whole town in an uproar over such news. Carissa could hear her heart thumping as Cameron replied.

"Nothing's definite, Mrs. Harbridge. You did agree to keep this secret."

Carissa's heart sank. What could Cameron be thinking? And Cameron looked so calm about it, keeping his hand in his pocket as he continued.

"We know the Everlys are expanding their business to contract with a cruise line. I asked the Harbridges if the Moss Hill Business Commission would be interested in supplying retail spaces on the cruise ships that carry items only found on Moss Hill. That way we increase the revenue of local businesses without necessarily increasing tourism in Moss Hill."

"That's brilliant," Mrs. Alcott exclaimed.

"We could start right away with a small supply, but I think it could expand quickly..." Mrs. Harbridge trailed off, walking with Mrs. Alcott toward the refreshments table.

"It really is a great idea," Carissa said.

"Thanks! I really need one right now."

He said it with some struggle in his voice. The moment passed briefly and he returned to handing out buttons with his "Camera Cam" smile. Yet, it had happened.

"What do you mean?" Carissa asked.

But Cameron changed the subject. "Reg came by City Hall while Maren went by the police station."

Carissa bit her lip. She knew what he would say next.

"It would have been nice to know that you were in Vale with all the commotion about kidnappers on the loose."

"I'm sorry. I didn't know about it until I was there and you know how the cell reception is out in the woods."

His head dropped to the side. "You could've called me when you were on your way home."

"I did answer your text," she said almost automatically.

"Saying, 'I'm fine' and 'goodnight' hours after I text you doesn't count. Carissa, you have to tell me everything, especially things that put you in danger. I know you're powerful, but you're not indestructible. I was minutes away from driving out there to find you."

Her cheeks reddened. She'd been talking with Alden and so caught up in other thoughts it hadn't occurred to her to call Cameron. Then, when she'd gotten home, she had been so caught up reading in her grandfather's study that she hadn't seen his text until near midnight. She realized her mistake.

"I promise I will call you next time. But, honestly, I was fine. Alden was with me."

Cameron reddened. "I'm glad you had someone you could rely on."

"What do you mean?" Carissa asked.

Was it another mistake to mention Alden? He had been one of Cameron's best friends when he was alive. He'd helped them both in tough situations. Cameron had never been bothered by that before.

He swallowed, then shook his head. "Nothing, never mind. I'm just glad you're all right."

"Cameron," Mr. Burrows, a stocky gentleman in an outdated business suit, called him away.

"Uh-oh, I should've insisted on talking to Tim Harbridge alone. His wife's going to tell the whole town before I have a chance to talk to Mr. Everly."

Cameron was not letting the argument get too far, for which Carissa was thankful. She tried to return the levity.

"I could've told you that," she said while attempting a smile.

He gave her a peck on the cheek and went as called. Carissa kept the hurt smile on her face as she watched him go. Then, breathing deep, she took in the scent of spring flowers. Sounds of laughter wafted through the April air. Scanning the churchyard with her eyes, she paused at a curious sight.

She just had to walk toward the out-of-place woman in dark colors sitting under the pavilion. Raven Corvus carried on quite the conversation—of all people with Timmy Harbridge Junior. Carissa listened.

"I help seelie fae all over the world. Humans too, when I can. Let's see, last time it was the Congo."

"What were you doing in the Congo?"

"Fighting off giant spiders known as the j'ba fofi."

"Giant spiders?" Timmy's eyebrows shot up.

"Six feet, easily, and aggressive. Why they could take a man and—"

"Timmy, why don't you go see how the nature faeries are doing?" Carissa intervened.

"Yeah, okay." Timmy got up slowly. He made it two steps before turning to look at Raven. "Did you win against the giant spiders?"

With a twinkle in her eye, she said, "I always win."

When Timmy had gone, Carissa restarted the conversation.

"Giant spiders? You do realize he's eight years old."

"Eight? Is anyone only eight years old? How incredibly young for a fighter."

"He's not a fighter—that's my point. He'll have nightmares about giant spiders if you tell him stories like that."

"Ah, but will he win? I think so. I can tell a strong spirit from a weak one. And don't tell me he's not a fighter after he led The Charge of the Schoolyard. He recounted the story to me himself."

Carissa squinted as she stared at this strange woman. Raven could tell about people, couldn't she? She had seen that Belkin was a troll right away. Could she just as easily tell how Mrs. O'Mally had been killed?

"You said yesterday that Mrs. O'Mally was murdered. How do you know?"

"She wreaked of changeling magic. Couldn't you tell? I'm always amazed that people can't tell."

Carissa frowned. That wasn't a real clue.

"Mrs. O'Mally was a troll," she clarified.

"Was she? Well, all the more reason to investigate."

Carissa crossed her arms. There was nothing strange about finding changeling magic on a troll. She could have used her magic in self-defense or to attack. At the least, she could have called on her powers as she struggled to survive. It was an unpleasant thought, but not extraordinary.

Carissa would have argued, but she wasn't going to get a clear answer. Raven was a curious mix of her two sisters. She had Miss Morgan's stubbornness and bluntness. She had Macara's penchant for cryptic statements. The question remained whether she had good intentions for Moss Hill.

"Never mind the changeling troll. That will get sorted out in time. You have far more important things to think about. Has Chaos been helpful to you?"

"Yes. Why did you send her to me? Why are you in Moss Hill?"

"It's time someone explained. My sisters didn't seem to have prepared you well for your fate."

"My fate or Moss Hill's?"

Raven smiled and fixed her eyes on Carissa. Then, she pointed to the bench next to her. "Sit. I don't want you fainting when I tell you."

Carissa could feel her skin tingling already. Was she finally going to get the full truth? Whatever Raven was going to tell her, it didn't seem good.

"Do you know who you are?"

That seemed like a strange question, but Carissa thought she knew what Raven was referring to. Months ago, Carissa had discovered her true heritage as a descendent of the Tuatha de Danann known as Queen Maeve. Carissa nodded.

"Good," Raven said. "Then you see why we put the spells over Moss Hill."

"Which spells are those?"

Raven counted on her fingers. "Let's see. MacLir's spell to hide the island from the outside world. Macara's spell to keep magic from being detected by the outside world. Babd, you called her Miss Morgan, I think; her spell to bind your family's Tuatha de Danann powers until you've each been found worthy of having them, which I think happened recently. And my spell."

"Which one is that?"

She leaned forward and whispered as if it were a great secret. "To undo all of the spells after two hundred years."

Then she sat up straight again and stared Carissa in the eye. There was a challenge in them. But what did she want Carissa to do?

"You don't understand," Raven said flatly. "Morgan said it was dangerous for the people in Moss Hill to know much about magic and about *you*, but I didn't think she'd deny you your entire history. It's wrong."

"Then tell me."

"Not here. The tourists have ears."

Raven stood up and stretched. Chaos, who had either been watching or sensed that Raven was leaving, flew straight to her. Her face and hands all full of chocolate, Chaos waved goodbye to Carissa. Then she pointed furiously toward the pens of pet rabbits. Raven laughed and headed in that direction.

Carissa waved back, knowing that they were no longer looking. It was all right, she couldn't manage as wholehearted a gesture as Chaos had. She was too busy wondering whether she could trust Raven or if the woman was just leading her down a rabbit hole. For now, safely seated at the outdoor table watching Raven walk away, she decided she'd reserve judgement until she learned more.

The bench she was seated on rattled. Carissa flinched before realizing that Barnaby and Holly had jumped onto the seat next to her. Barnaby took off his signature green hat.

Carissa's eyes lit up. "Barnaby, Holly, are you all right? I'm so sorry I wasn't there for you yesterday."

"I should've known that Raven was in town. She always brings trouble with her," Holly said.

"We were waiting for her to leave," Barnaby added.

Holly snorted. "*You* were. I don't have a problem telling the old bat exactly what I think."

"I'm an old crow, not a bat," Raven called out.

It was a wonder she could still hear them. Everyone in the churchyard must have heard her. A few people turned around. Barnaby paled. Raven went right back to watching Chaos pet bunnies. Holly reddened, but kept a stubborn eye on her.

"Did she say what she was doing here?" Barnaby asked.

"Not yet. All I know is she says she's here to protect Moss Hill."

Holly's voice softened to a whisper. "Protect it from whatever she's brought to it. *'The Raven's crow is a call to arms.'* That's a well-known fact of history."

History. That was what Raven promised to tell her. Would she leave that part out? Carissa shuddered and rubbed her arms to brush off her sudden chill.

"Have you heard anything about the tourists who kidnapped you?"

It was Barnaby's turn to shudder. "No. It does nothing for my sleep knowing they're out there."

"Relax, Barn, Macara's back. We've got more than one Tuatha de Danann protecting us now," Holly said.

"That's fine for you. You've got one right in your own home. What have I got? A house full of humans is not like having a powerful being around."

"Nonsense. You've got one right across the street."

"What's that?"

Carissa raised her eyebrows and shook her head. Barnaby did not know she was part Tuatha de Danann. Holly took the hint.

"Uh, a powerful fae, I mean."

"Oh yeah, Carissa. That's true. Best keep an eye out on my home and shop, Cari."

"I'll be vigilant, I promise. Can you tell me how you were kidnapped?"

Holly said, "I'd gone to Gooseberry in the morning, and at lunch I took over the cinnamon rolls I'd bought to Barnaby's so that we could eat together."

"We talked a while," Barnaby said.

"Argued is more like it," Holly corrected, "but that's beside the point."

"The next thing we knew, we were in a room at the hotel being stuffed into duffle bags and taken out to the forest," Barnaby said.

"So this was around noon?"

Holly and Barnaby bobbed their heads.

"And you think the kidnappers were tourists?"

"We're sure," Barnaby said.

"We saw their faces. They weren't concerned because they said they'd be off on the next ferry," Holly said.

Carissa ran a hand through her red hair. Would the kidnappers still try to leave on a ferry knowing the fae were looking for them? If they didn't take the ferry, would they continue to stay at the only hotel in town? It should be easy to catch them, given that Moss Hill was such a small town.

"The police or the sidhe will find them. Don't worry," Carissa assured. She invited them to her parents' home for the welcoming party. They gave a resounding yes. Then, Holly stood up.

"Well, we're back and we're safe. That's all that matters. We'll see you tonight," she said.

Barnaby stood as well. "Right. Might as well enjoy the festivities. Have a good day, Carissa."

Barnaby repositioned his hat and followed behind the bean tighe. They headed straight for the Gooseberry tent for a serving of chit-chat and chocolate. Carissa decided to take Barnaby's advice. There was nothing she could do at the moment about Raven or Mrs. O'Mally. She might as well enjoy the day.

Chapter 8

Tempting Fate

There was nothing left to enjoy once she spotted Belkin setting up his *Believe in Belkin* signs all over the grass. Carissa waited for the potato sack race contestants to pass her and then took a shortcut toward the churchyard entrance where Belkin was handing the signs to volunteers. Father Quinn got there first.

"Sir, I'm afraid you cannot put your signs here. This is a privately-owned park on church grounds. I must ask you to stop."

"If you'll look carefully, Father, you'll see we're placing them on the grass belonging to the sidewalk. It's public property and I have a permit." Belkin unfolded a yellow paper from his breast pocket.

The Father glanced at the paper, lifted his hat and walked away. But Carissa would not let him off so easily. She'd made it past the welcome booth and was about to give him a piece of her mind when the most unexpected sight stopped in her tracks. Darting behind a tree, she looked again.

There he was: Parker Greer. Could he be the other prisoner Warren mentioned having to attend to back on the ship? He had tried to poison Belkin with a bad luck charm at Christmas. His unfortunate actions had inadvertently led to the death of an elfkin. It wasn't the same as murder, but shouldn't it require a sentence of more than four months? And why was Belkin talking to him at all, given that he was the target of Parker's schemes? It made no sense.

Father Quinn walked by. He stopped and raised an eyebrow upon seeing Carissa. She shifted her weight, crossed her arms, and leaned against the tree, trying to look nonchalant.

"Carissa?"

She ignored the raised syllable at the end of her name and smiled.

"Father, lovely day, isn't it? Everyone is really enjoying themselves."

He hesitated, then apparently deciding all was well, responded, "Yes, yes everything turned out nicely. Good day."

He tipped his hat to her and continued. She kept her position, trying not to look like she was spying. Using her elf-ears to overhear as much of the conversation as she could, she glanced occasionally at the pair but kept an otherwise low profile. From the sound of it, Belkin wasn't too pleased with Parker's sudden appearance.

"What do you want?" Belkin said as he hammered a sign into the ground.

"I think you know," Parker replied.

He kept his hands in his pockets as he gave a casual shrug. If he was going for anonymity, he missed the mark. His sunglasses and hat did nothing to hide his identity. A pink pocket square sat pretentiously in the jacket of his gray suit, and his shoes appeared recently shined.

Belkin held the hammer between them. "I met you yesterday out of sheer curiosity. Now that I've heard you out, I'm not interested."

"I can make sure you win this election in a landslide."

Belkin smirked. "What makes you think I can't do that myself?"

Parker stepped closer. "Those spells are not regular magic. They take more than just your...natural abilities."

"I didn't use magic to win the first time and I don't need it this time."

"Are you sure?" Parker asked. He took the pocket square and flicked it open, handing it to Belkin, adding, "You're sweating."

Belkin waved the hammer. "Leave or I'll call the sidhe to arrest you again."

Parker put his hands up and stepped back. Tucking the handkerchief in his breast pocket, he swiveled on his heels. On his first step forward, he locked eyes with Carissa. She ducked back.

Closing her eyes, she winced at her own carelessness. Then, taking a couple breaths, she reassured herself that maybe Parker hadn't noticed her. It was possible to look right at someone without really registering that they were there. She came away from the oak slowly and to the other side of it.

"I know you're behind the tree, Carissa."

She let out her breath. So, she wasn't spy material. Turning around, she came face to face with the former jailbird. Parker smiled.

"It's good to see you, Carissa."

Crossing her arms, she replied, "Why are you here?"

"I was a member of this congregation. The event is open to everyone."

"I mean in Moss Hill. Weren't you serving your sentence in Tir-Na-Nog?"

"Lovely place. If the king hadn't insisted on overseeing my sentence himself, I'd have been stuck in a sidhe dungeon in Vale. Can you imagine?"

She didn't respond. His smile waned.

"I did my time. I'm a free man now. But, to answer your question, I'm planning on leaving Moss Hill. Just as soon as I collect everything that belongs to me, I'll be gone. How does that sound?"

"It sounds like it shouldn't take long."

"It depends. There's something in Moss Hill of great personal value to me. As soon as I have it, you'll never see me again."

Promises, promises, she thought. Parker was playing a game. He had two qualities that she knew of: coveting power and manipulating others to get it. Carissa would not take part in either.

"Just don't go near Maren or Cam," she said before turning and walking away.

"Or you'll cast a spell on me?" he called out.

She didn't give him the satisfaction of replying. Without turning around, she made it back to the center of the fun and games. She needed a break now. Barnaby and Holly had the right idea, going over to the Gooseberry Bakery tent. Maren hadn't left it all morning. Either she was still on duty or the sweets were too good to leave.

"You look like you need a cupcake."

"Forget the cup. I'll take the whole cake."

"That bad?" Maren said, handing her the largest chocolate cupcake she could find.

Carissa took it, gratefully. She pulled the wrapper away from the edges.

"Don't be upset, Maren, but I just saw Parker."

Maren's fingernails tapped the table.

"Isn't he in jail or a dungeon or whatever the sidhe call it?" she asked.

"His sentence is over."

"Four months. That's nothing."

"He didn't technically try to commit murder. It was just a bad luck spell."

"Still, you'd think he'd get more than that."

"Are you, all right?" Carissa asked.

Maren's eyes scanned the pastries. She swiped a scone and took a large bite, chewed, swallowed, and sighed.

"Honestly, it doesn't matter if he's back. I have Reg now, and friends, and two great careers. I don't even have time to think of old boyfriends."

Carissa smiled and took a bite of the chocolate cupcake. The perfect mix of gooey and fluffiness ended Carissa's worries. Maren diverted the conversation.

"So, have you seen Jane today?"

Carissa raised an eyebrow. Maren leaned forward with a looked that screamed scandal.

"She's here with that druid from the boat."

"Warren?" Carissa asked.

Maren nodded, then jerked her head to the right, looking past Carissa to the egg painting booth. Sure enough, there was Jane, helping a group of children while Warren watched over their creations. He smiled at her when she looked at him. When she looked away, he scratched his ear and raised an eyebrow at the eggs, looking very much out of place.

"Well, that's unexpected," Carissa remarked.

"Even stranger is what happened to Barnaby and Holly," Maren said.

Carissa put a hand up. "I already know. I've invited them to my parents' cottage in Vale tonight. You should come along, Maren."

"Love to. Can I bring Reg?"

Carissa agreed with a nod. "Where is he?"

"Talking politics with Cam. He's really enjoying it."

"Cam said that he—"

"Carissa," Holly dashed into the tent. She talked at a hundred words a second. "Where is Varick? Oh, never mind."

She disappeared before Carissa had even processed what she was asking. She and Maren looked at each other. Dropping the cupcake and the scone, the two of them chased after her.

"There," Maren said, spotting Holly and Barnaby gibbering to an annoyed-looking sidhe.

Carissa and Maren soon joined them at the refreshments stand.

"I saw her by the raffle bin," Barnaby said.

"What was she doing?" Varick did not look at Barnaby as he answered.

"She was, uh, filling out a raffle card. She dropped some on the ground and was bending to pick them up. Well, how do I know what she was really doing? That could have been a cover!"

Varick raised an eyebrow but still did not break his gaze with whatever he was staring at.

Carissa and Maren tried to look in the same direction. They raised their own eyebrows at each other when they saw where he was looking.

"I know how strange it sounds, kidnapping us one day and participating in a church raffle the next," Holly started.

"You're probably mistaken," Varick said.

A frown began on his face and only deepened when Carissa glanced between him and the object of his attention. Warren used a napkin to wipe paint off Jane's nose. She smiled and said something, probably a "thank you."

"It's the same woman who kidnapped us!" Barnaby wrung his hat the way Carissa imagined he'd like to wring Varick's neck.

Still, Varick did not look away from Jane. Maren cleared her throat loudly. Varick seemed to snap out of it. He looked between Maren and Carissa, whose arms had crossed and lips had thinned into a reprimand.

Varick relented, "Is the man with her?"

"No," Holly said.

"And you're certain it's the same woman?"

"Well, I didn't see her. Barnaby?"

Barnaby's head bobbed side to side and he stood on tiptoes to see through the crowd.

Holly whispered to Barnaby, "Maybe he's right. We only saw them in the evening as it was getting dark."

"Stop!" Barnaby yelled suddenly.

Small as he was, Barnaby was a quick footed leprechaun. He ran before any of them could catch him.

Varick growled. Then he, Holly, Maren, and Carissa followed. Barnaby dove under the egg painting table, pulling at the plastic table cloth and causing several of the eggs to topple. Several of the kids began to cry.

Warren leapt right into action. He couldn't have known what was happening exactly, but it was clear that a mad leprechaun was giving chase to something.

"Stop! Stop!" Barnaby yelled as weaved under tables and through legs to get to the kidnappers.

Varick and Warren leapt over them at a faster rate. They looked at one another and each increased speed. Carissa shook her head. Fae or druid, did all men treat everything as a competition?

She and Maren were too polite to dash over booths. This also meant that they arrived at the raffle booth slower than the rest of the group.

"Over there, in the yellow shirt!"

Warren unsheathed a wand and shot at a woman near where Barnaby was pointing. Screams flew through the air. The woman lifted and pulled back as if thrown toward them. Warren guided her into a chair. The woman struggled against magical ropes, glowing orange with greater intensity as she resisted.

"Is this the woman you're looking for?" Warren asked.

The woman's eyes grew incredibly large. Carissa couldn't blame her given the druid and sidhe both staring at her. Though, as it turned out, Varick was glaring more at Warren than anyone else.

"That's Mrs. Walsh from the flower shop on Third Street." Maren tried to stand between him.

"She's not the one I was pointing at!" Barnaby said.

"Let her go," Carissa said.

Warren lifted the hazel wand and sheathed it at his waist. The orange beams ceased. The woman sat still, too terrified to move. Carissa helped Mrs. Walsh up, offering a "we're sorry" as the frightened woman wobbled away.

"There was another woman in yellow. Couldn't you see where I was pointing?"

"Foolish leprechaun," Varick muttered.

"But she's getting away!"

Holly gave Barnaby's shoulder a light thwack. He rubbed it but didn't say another word. Varick turned around and glared at the crowd.

"There's nothing to see," he stated harshly.

Carissa stepped into his line of sight and tilted her chin. He caught sight of her and someone else behind her. Jane, it turned out. Her brows knitted and her lips turned downward. Warren moved closer to ask if she was all right. Varick's voice dropped to a tone Carissa hadn't heard before.

"Resume your merriment," he added more calmly.

"What's going on?" Cameron jogged up next to them.

Carissa shook her head. "False alarm."

Cameron nodded. He turned to the crowd.

"Just a little mishap, everyone. So sorry for the interruption. If we could just have a few volunteers to clean up this area.... We'll do the raffle in about fifteen minutes."

As Cameron continued to pacify the crowd, Barnaby tugged on Carissa's sleeve.

"You have to believe me, Carissa, she was here."

Carissa looked between the mothers and fathers and children and townsfolk. There were so many it was difficult to make out who Barnaby had seen, but she was certain of one thing.

"I believe you," she said to Barnaby.

There had been another person in yellow at the boat yesterday.

***

CARISSA DID NOT escape the scene unscathed. Paint splattered everywhere after parties ran through Jane's booth. While Varick had been clever enough to evade the mess, and Maren far enough behind to have missed the spill, Carissa had run right through as the various colors flew through the air.

She was careful to keep from touching the walls as she entered the church, all the while dabbing herself with the towels Mrs. Alcott had been kind enough to lend her. By the time she'd entered the basement, the once pink towel had taken on a purple hue.

"Great," she muttered to herself as she entered the restroom.

She looked like one of the multi-colored eggs the youngest of the children had painted. Thankfully, most of it came off as she splashed her face with water from the sink. Color immediately returned to her face when she saw a shadow behind her in the mirror.

Spinning around, she said, "Who's there?"

"Just me," a woman's voice called. "I'm a mess." Jane emerged from one of the stalls and walked up to the sink next to her. "Thank goodness I brought an extra blouse. I knew the children could be messy, though I hadn't imagined what actually happened."

It looked like Jane had already cleaned her face and hands. She began adjusting her disheveled hair. After a moment, she raised an eyebrow. Realizing how tense she must have looked, Carissa relaxed.

"Sorry, I'm a little jumpy."

"I don't blame you. Warren told me about Mrs. O'Mally, and Holly just explained about the kidnapping."

Carissa held the door so that Jane could exit first. Carissa threw the towels in a hamper outside the restroom and walked up the stairs with Jane. She was too curious not to follow the druidess out of the church.

"I noticed Warren has been sticking close by you all day."

"He's taken an interest in my training. He wants to convince Macara that he's the best one to teach me druidic magic."

"And how do you feel about that?"

Jane stopped just inside the church doors. "He's interesting. He wants me to go with him—traveling. I've always wanted to see the world outside of Moss Hill."

"So, are you thinking of going with him?"

"I can't. Moss Hill has always had a druid or druidess watching over it. I petitioned the Sidhe Council to allow me to leave the role to someone else, but the only other human on the island with magic is still a child and…"

"And?"

"Well, you, but Raven thinks you're needed somewhere else. They're still debating what your role should be."

"Why am I not involved in this decision?"

"Neither of us have any real say. I wasn't called on to make the decision. I was called on to investigate O'Mally's death."

"I can help you with that."

"There's nothing to do. I've seen the crime scene. It seems to have been an accident."

"Have you talked to Raven about it?"

"Macara said not to take Raven too seriously."

Carissa bit her lip. Everyone seemed to be saying that. Maybe she shouldn't be listening to her either.

"Do you think Raven is right that there was a murder?" Jane asked.

"I think it's best to keep an open mind," Carissa replied.

Jane agreed. "I suppose anything is possible in Moss Hill."

Except the things we really want. Carissa couldn't help but think that the council was placing Jane in her position. Jane, who wanted to be free of Moss Hill, was stuck here to protect it. And Carissa, who wanted nothing more than to stay and protect her beloved town; what would they decide for her fate?

Chapter 9

Beyond the Vale

This afternoon, Vale was calm. It was too early for the usual tranquility of a town settling in for the night. There should have been vendors in the central square trading produce and goods. There should have been shoppers chatting and sidhe guards watching over the crowd. Instead, the wind wailed in Carissa's ears and no other sights could be seen or sounds heard.

She clutched Cameron's arm as they walked down the road.

"Where is everyone?" Carissa asked.

"Maybe your parents invited the whole town," Cam answered in a light-hearted tone, but he looked around apprehensively as they turned off the main path.

Carissa's parents' home lay alone at the end of a short path. She'd never thought about its location before. Now, it seemed to sit deliberately on the edge of town beside the boulders. Being a cottage, it was not as large or prestigious as that of Head Elf Roland's home, nor was it as superb as the splendor of the sidhe mounds, but with the faerie lights in the garden, the table extended with a long, white clothed draped over it, and fine sparkling silver atop, the backyard made a fine atmosphere for a welcome home party.

Several sidhe and elf residents of Vale were in attendance. Among them, Head Elf Roland stood near the fountain in deep discussion with the captain of the king's ship. Cameron joined them, but Carissa was drawn to another guest. Varick stood away from everyone, leaning against the boulders. Nearly everything about him was cross, from his arms to his attitude.

His eyes followed Jane, who stood conversing with Hela beside a small table set out with pre-dinner snacks and elderberry juice. His stare moved inches away to where, unsurprisingly, Warren was filling two glasses with elderberry juice.

Carissa excused herself from a perfectly polite conversation with Cameron and Roland to open a dialogue with a jealous sidhe captain. She found a spot beside Varick and rested against the rock.

"Stare any longer and you'll burn a hole right through him."

Carissa could hear how much she sounded like Nan after the words flew out of her mouth. Varick's gaze shifted sideways, then back to Warren. She would have left him alone, but the only thing worse than an angry sidhe was a miserable one.

"A word of advice?"

He didn't say anything, but he didn't walk away either.

"When you love someone, you want them to be happy."

He uncrossed his arms and looked at Carissa.

"I want nothing less for Jane than her happiness."

"Even if it's not with you?"

Varick looked away. His eyes found Warren again.

"She is free to fall in love with anyone—but not with him."

"Why?"

"The Druvall family is deceitful at best and dangerous at worst."

"I doubt the king would hire him if he wasn't trustworthy."

"Many kings have hired them. Most have regretted it."

"Why? What have they done?"

"In the last few generations, they became Maeve's personal protectors. Some say they were not loyal to Maeve, which is why she died. Others say they lost their status and became rogues after she died. Either way, since then, they have no loyalty to anyone. They stole the fairy flag from the MacLeod family, trained the cu sith to become hounds of war, and became mercenaries for hire to the highest bidder—seelie or unseelie."

"If they have no moral standards, why would any seelie hire them?"

"Their moral standard is the contract. They fulfill all of their contracts. If a king hires a Druvall to kill a peasant and a peasant pays well enough to kill a king, both king and peasant will die as written in the contract."

"So why would King Finvarra trust him enough to give him a rank and title?"

"Whatever wrong the Druvalls do, they remain among the most skilled druids on earth."

"Varick, I don't doubt what you're saying, and I think it's right to be a little cautious of Warren. But I also know Prince Zephyr is the one responsible for the king's fleets. He's not the kind to trust people with shady characters. Maybe we should get to know Warren before pre-judging him. People are not defined by their family lines."

Varick couldn't know how much she wanted, and needed, him to believe that last statement. If the sidhe like him could have so much anger for a family who worked for Queen Maeve, then how much more would they hate Carissa for being a direct descendant? If he found out, would Varick think of her the same way he did Warren?

"To the sidhe, there is nothing higher than family."

"And if you met him and found that he was a man of honor?"

"He's not."

"You're saying that because he's getting close to Jane."

"Yes, I am," Varick admitted.

Carissa raised an eyebrow. He was openly admitting to jealousy? His green eyes were almost glowing as he looked at her.

He clarified. "Feelings aside, she is the druidess of Moss Hill. You're forgetting that I'm a captain tasked with protecting Vale and Moss Hill. Raven Corvus believes there has been a murder. Warren refuses to investigate. Why?"

"He and the elf guard believed there was no evidence of foul play. And...well, Raven hasn't always been the most trustworthy."

"She seeks war, she does not create it," Varick said.

That wasn't true according to everyone she'd spoken to so far, but she wasn't going to push the issue with Varick. He was trying to make a point. She had to hear it before she could judge it.

"What are you saying—that Warren killed Mrs. O'Mally on purpose?"

"He admits to firing at her."

"There was evidence of a fight. Jane agreed that it was likely an accident. The prisoner tried to run and he tried to recapture her."

"Or he tried to kill a prisoner and she fought back. Warren may be manipulating Jane. He seems to have done so with the elf guards, too. They battled just as he turned the corner to the stairs. Is it not convenient that no one could see them at that point?"

"If Mrs. O'Mally had wanted to escape, it would have been the best time for her to try to lose the guards."

"Both are plausible, which is why I haven't arrested him yet."

"If you're right, then why just watch him? Why not talk with him to try to find out more?"

"I cannot approach him. If the prince has named him head of the elf guards on a royal vessel, then he is my superior in rank."

"Well, he's not mine. I think I'll ask him a question or two."

Varick gave a sarcastic grunt she took to mean *good luck with that.* Carissa ignored him and walked to the refreshments table. Warren was walking away with the two drinks when she stopped him.

"Warren, or Mr. Druvall, sorry, I'm not sure how you prefer to be addressed."

He looked at her as if waiting for her to get on with her point.

"I had a few questions about Mrs. O'Mally."

There was a light tapping on a glass that beckoned Warren's attention. He and Carissa both looked at the origin of the sound. Sal set down the fork and glass.

Head Elf Roland stood near the center of the table and held up a glass. The attendees gathered at the table. Warren and Jane stood in front of chairs opposite where Rolin was standing. Hela and her husband, Fen, took places near the head elf, her father. Carissa walked closer.

"Welcome home to the travelers who have returned from Tir-Na-Nog, and to those who have just arrived in Moss Hill for the first time."

Heads bowed toward the captain of the king's ship and Warren. More than a few sidhe and elves narrowed their eyes or took sideways glances at the druid.

Roland continued. "Long life and prosperity to our hosts, Dorian and Kaley Shae."

Sal rushed through the crowd, providing cups of the elderberry juice for the toast. All who had glasses raised them and called out, "Long life and prosperity," in response.

"Now, I believe my daughter and son-in-law have an announcement of their own."

Fen took his wife's hand. "We are so very pleased to announce—"

"We're expecting a child!" Hela squealed.

Applause exploded around the table. Carissa and Cameron came together to join them. With a hug and a kiss for the expectant mother, and a handshake for the new father-to-be, the pair offered congratulations. Then, they sat at the table beside their friends and waited for the rest of the guests to be seated.

Reg and Maren sat opposite Cameron and Carissa. Though, Maren stood up again a few seconds after everyone was seated. All eyes turned to the curious human with the upraised glass.

"Everyone, Reg has an announcement and he'd like you all to be the first to hear it."

Maren's smile burst joy like a broken dam. Reg touched her elbow and urged her to sit down. Carissa's interest piqued and she titled her head in anticipation of the announcement.

"Now might not be the right time," Reg said softly.

"Nonsense. It's perfect." She straightened the pocket square in Reg's maroon suit.

Reg stood and took off his glasses. Wiping them with his suit jacket, he began shakily, "I spoke with the city council members yesterday and today, and, well, I suppose I should just say it: as of this afternoon, I'll be throwing my hat into the ring."

"Sorry?" Cameron asked.

"He's running for mayor!" Maren clamped a hand on her mouth, then removed it. "Sorry, I'm just so excited."

Carissa opened and closed her mouth. What was she supposed to say to that? Reginald wasn't even a Mossie!

"It's a challenging role," Cameron said.

"Yes, I know. But I have a wealth of information about the law from my dad's firm, and I've got extensive knowledge and now experience, too, with the fae. Plus, MacLir wants me to stick close to Moss Hill. What better way than as mayor?"

Maren's lips couldn't have curved more upward if she tried. Her smile wavered as she caught sight of Carissa's face. There was no way she could have missed the *how could you?* in Carissa's eyes.

As the congratulations went around the table, Carissa took Cameron's hand in reassurance. The four of them glanced awkwardly at one another until the table eased into individual conversations. Then, Maren leaned forward to speak.

"I know what you're thinking. And Cameron, I know you had your sights set on being mayor. But, you yourself said the office might be dangerous," Maren said.

"You said that?" Carissa asked.

"Yes, I mean, well, in passing." He whispered to her, "I didn't mean he should run against me."

"Dangerous or not, we don't want Belkin back in the office, do we? I have some of MacLir's magic. I can use it for my protection while in office," Reg remarked.

He looked guilty when he said it, which only told Carissa that he knew how wrong this was. If he wanted to be mayor, why couldn't he wait until Cameron's term was up? Wasn't there an unwritten rule of friendship applicable here?

"Or you could use MacLir's power to protect whomever gets elected," Cameron murmured.

"I'll protect you and so will Macara and Raven," Carissa responded.

Carissa purposefully turned her head to listen to the conversation Raven was having with Hela.

"So, you lived in Mexico?" Hela was asking.

Chaos, who'd come to her in a box with a note and a chocolate cosmos plant, spent her first few days in Moss Hill homesick and longing for the blue skies of her native land. Ms. Corvus had sprawled a difficult-to-read address on the package, but the country was unmistakable. It was Mexico that Chaos had missed.

"I'm entitled to a vacation now and again," Raven responded.

"You were vacationing in Mexico? Is that where you found the little faerie, Chaos?" Hela knew enough about the package to be curious about the sender.

"Found Chaos? I made Chaos."

"You usually do," Macara whispered as she took a sip of elderberry juice.

"What do you mean you made Chaos?" Carissa asked.

Now, that whole table section of the table was listening in.

"It started with the plant. I was craving chocolate and reading about an extinct plant that smelled of the heavenly scent. I needed an addition to my garden, so I recreated it."

"You created the modern chocolate cosmos plant?" Carissa asked.

"What one will do when craving chocolate," Raven joked.

"But the plant is inedible," Maren said.

"To humans. I don't have your limitations, but still, I didn't eat it. The scent is enough."

"How did you create it?" Carissa asked.

"A bit of magic can do marvelous things. I overshot, though. Put too much of myself into it, and there was Chaos."

"You made a whole new nature faerie when you made a new type of plant? That's incredible!" Reg said.

"But every chocolate cosmos we have today comes from one single plant in 1902," Carissa countered.

Carissa had done her research on the plant since Chaos's arrival.

"I allowed the humans to take a tuber off the plant to have their own pieces. Don't worry, I told them not to eat them."

"Wait," Maren said, shaking her head as if to wrap her mind around it. "If Chaos was born in 1902, she's over a hundred years old!"

"Your point?"

Carissa and Maren looked at each other. Despite Reg's direct competition with Cameron, Carissa's first reaction was to share the shock with her best friend. It was difficult to break a friendship that had lasted since high school. Even more impossible to believe was that the childish nature faerie, Chaos, was far older than either of them—it made two years as mayor seem like a blip in time.

"Speaking of Chaos," Carissa finally snapped herself out of shock enough to recall a curious event, "Raven, I want to ask you about something that happened to Chaos in October."

Raven nodded. "Her wings turned black."

"Yes! How did you know?"

"She's part of the chocolate cosmos. She follows the cycle of the plant. As it turns black, her wings turn black."

"But her powers—she had enough magic to stand up to an ankou!"

"Unsurprising. She grows more and less powerful according to the plant."

"If something were to happen to the plant—"

"Replant the tubers every year. Take care that she's always around a chocolate cosmos. Her powers and her being come from the plant."

"That's why she didn't want to be separated from the chocolate cosmos when she first came to Moss Hill," Maren said.

"All nature faeries need nature, not just Chaos," Holly interjected.

The conversation was hijacked by the two leprechauns as Barnaby joined in. "The kidnappers used a nature faerie to knock us out. Faerie dust is powerful, you know?"

"Oh, Barn, we've already told everyone the story. I don't think they want to hear about the kidnapping again," Holly said in a tone that implied she very much wanted to talk about the kidnapping.

"But you recalled something important, my dear, and I thought we were going to tell them."

"Tell us what?" Raven asked.

Holly opted to look past Raven to Macara when answering. "They had some kind of book with them. I think it was called *The Faerie*...uh..."

Barnaby filled in the blanks. "*Secrets of the Faerie People.*"

Reg coughed and reached for his drink.

"Reg?" Maren asked.

"He's turning red. Someone help him," Barnaby exclaimed.

"I'm okay," Reg squeaked out.

Maren patted his back, but Carissa wasn't about to give him the same sympathy.

"You recognize the title."

"I…uh…" He tugged at his collar.

"You what?" Carissa asked.

"I need a drink."

He grabbed the nearest pitcher of elderberry juice, topped off his cup, and drank. Then, he reached again to refill.

"Don't they have anything stronger?"

"Reg, what on earth is wrong?" Maren asked.

Cameron held down the pitcher until Reg let go.

"Spill it," Cameron ordered.

Reg set down his cup.

"All right." He took off his glasses and pinched the bridge of his nose. "When I first came to Moss Hill, you know I had an interest in the fae. I was writing a book—"

"You wrote the book!" Barnaby's finger accused him before he'd even begun.

"Whoa, Barnaby. Let him finish," Cam said.

Barnaby quieted, but the way he clutched his fork while staring at the space between Reg's eyes made Carissa fear he might launch it.

Reg put on his glasses and swallowed.

"It was before MacLir hired me—before I knew any of you. I talked to a publisher, even sent the first version of the manuscript to one, but once I realized what MacLir was actually proposing, I canceled the deal. No one should have published it without my consent."

"Obviously someone did."

"Well, then at least it's the wrong version. It was before I actually knew the real facts about the fae."

"Wrong version." Barnaby grunted. "I'll say."

"I updated it. I even…oh no."

Mid-sentence, Reg rested his forehead against his palm.

"Oh no what?" Carissa asked.

"I may have added some spells I found in the Moss Hill Library." He added more forcefully, "But, I absolutely did not send it to the publisher. I left the updated version with Declan Greer for safekeeping."

"The librarian?" Maren asked.

Reg gulped. "The first time I was in Moss Hill, I already had an agent interested in the book. The agent, Sam Haley, told me the book would be more interesting if I had first person accounts to back up my theories. So I came to the island and met MacLir and, well, you know that story."

Carissa did, in fact, know that story well. She'd been there when Chaos exorcised the spirit of the old ankou out of Reg's body. More precisely, she'd been his target. But MacLir erased that part of Reg's memory until he was sure the nosy would-be lawyer with a hobby in fae-spotting, and apparently writing, could be trustworthy.

"MacLir told Greer to give me whatever books he had on the fae. I went to the Moss Hill Library a few times and Greer helped me with my research. I still had the original journal I'd written the book in, so I just added to it. I didn't know it then, but MacLir was preparing me for my work with all of you."

"I went back to England and canceled the deal with agent, quit my father's firm, and went to work with MacLir. Then, I came back to Moss Hill under MacLir's orders. I kept working on the book during my free time, but I was going to donate the updated version to Moss Hill. I thought it might help people understand the fae better. I wasn't trying to out anyone's secrets, I swear."

"Maybe Greer had other plans," Cameron said.

"I don't think so," Reg replied. He took another drink and ran a hand through his hair. "I don't know. It's possible. I left the book and all my notes with Greer for safekeeping before I went to Tir-Na-Nog."

"I'll go to the library tomorrow, then I'll call the publisher. My father's firm will have a perfect case to sue if they published the book without even informing me."

"Call the publisher first. Carissa and I will go to the library with you," Maren said.

Carissa was a bit taken aback. "Sure."

"Uh, Cari," Cameron turned to whisper to her, "I don't think that's such a—"

"I do not see how a publisher does anything for the fae being targeted here and now," Roland said.

Reg gulped. "They'll recall the copies or something. Don't worry, I'll take care of everything."

"You'd better," Roland replied.

Carissa flinched. She'd forgotten the other fae at the table were even listening to the conversation. All eyes were on Reginald. More than a few were glaring, including Varick.

Roland sounded serious as he continued, "If you do not correct it, this will be a matter to take to the councils of both the elves and sidhe."

Reg's panic made Carissa forget her anger and moved her to sympathy. His mistake was going to land him in trouble with the entire village of Vale. He wasn't likely to win a mayoral election now, but even if he wanted to stay in Moss Hill, he was going to need all the help he could get.

Chapter 10

Ocean Reaper

Hela excelled in hysterics. At the end of the evening, when the sidhe and elves in attendance were making their exit, the elf-maiden took her cloak from her host's hands and stated loudly that she hoped no humans were lurking in the shadows armed with knowledge about how to catch a faerie. Her husband, Fen, assured her that she would be safe as long as he was with her. Her father, Roland, ordered Sal to stay behind and make certain Fen's statement proved true. Well after the head elf had gone, Hela decided she'd made enough of the dramatic goodbyes, and she, Fen, and Sal went on their way.

The second they were gone, Raven said, "Druid Druvall, if you'll be kind enough to see Jane home, we'll join you in Moss Hill shortly."

Warren looked as if he wanted to argue, but his captain also rose with the offer to see Jane at least to the edge of Vale. Both bowed. When they left, Chaos gathered everyone together into the living room.

"You all know why you're here."

"No, they don't, Raven. The council didn't permit us to talk about it." Macara sounded very much like an older sister.

"Well, they should've figured it out," Raven said.

"You want to assign us our roles? The council ruled that Jane should be the protector of Moss Hill and I should be some kind of ambassador to other fae around the world, just like what my mother does. Is that what you'd like to tell us?"

Raven cackled, "She's perfect! See, I told you she would be."

"Yes and no," Macara said. "We did have to inform you of the council's will. They wish for Raven to train you and I will train Jane in her duties, but that was not all that we have to tell you."

"I hope it's that we have a choice."

"Is there a choice that's better than the one the council made?" Raven asked.

"I'm not an ambassador," Carissa said.

"Neither am I," Carissa's mother said. "That's your father's title. I was a spy. The fae always thought I was human, so I'd stay in the background on our trips to fae lands. I'd gather intel and send it to Macara, but I've been found out."

She sounded mournful. Her father took her mother's hands. Tears stung Carissa's eyes as she saw her mother holding back her own. She was grateful to feel Cameron's arm around her.

"What happened?" Carissa asked gently.

"Your powers were revealed and the unseelie got word of your being a Tuatha de Danann," Raven said.

"It doesn't matter," said Macara. "Carissa, I know I gave you the hope that you would be protector of

Moss Hill, but given what else we learned in Tir-Na-Nog, I think the council's ruling is best."

"What else did you learn?" Cameron asked.

"That my cousin is a traitor," Carissa's mother said.

Reg put it more clearly, "Your grandfather was one of seven children of Maeve. Most of her descendants have either chosen to stay in Hy Brasil or to give up their powers and blend in with humans. But there is one who chose to continue your great-grandmother's legacy."

"What legacy is that?" Maren asked.

Carissa had read enough from her grandfather's study to know the answer to that question.

She said, "To establish a kingdom over the human world. She wanted nothing less than for the Tuatha de Danann to rule over earth and all of the people—fae and human alike."

"Your cousin was determined to find Moss Hill and recruit you or defeat you," said her mother.

"So, why not get the other Tuatha de Danann to help?"

"They don't interfere with the world. They're not supposed to be here at all. Only MacLir, Macara, and Raven are allowed to travel to the human and fae realms as long as their experiment is running," Carissa's mother explained.

"Their experiment?" Cameron said.

"Moss Hill. They convinced the Tuatha de Danann that they could, eventually, create a world where fae and humans could be together. Your grandfather led the experiment before he was killed."

"Moss Hill is an experiment?" Cameron was still wrapping his mind around that.

"One MacLir would like to keep running." Reg raised his brow as he looked at Cameron. There was some unspoken implication he wanted Cameron to see. What was it? That MacLir wanted to keep Moss Hill running—personally? Did he want Reg to run for mayor so that he could be sure all final decisions were left for him? Maybe Reg's running for the position wasn't really his idea at all.

Macara said, "If the unseelie prove that humans and fae can't live together, the Tuatha de Danann will rule for all of their own kind to go back to Hy Brasil."

"All Tuatha de Danann?" Carissa asked without hesitation. Cameron, Maren, and Reg all looked to Macara with open mouthed stares. They all knew what she was really asking: Would Carissa also have to leave the human realm?

"Maeve didn't follow that law. The unseelie who support her legacy don't follow any laws," Raven explained.

Macara added, "Without a place like Moss Hill, without *us*, there's a chance the unseelie will have what they want: a world where the humans are ruled by fae."

The words were followed by a pounding sound outside that scared Maren straight to her feet.

"What was that?" Maren asked.

The door flew open. Pale-faced and shaking, Hela entered only to faint in her husband's arms. Fen woke her gently and guided her to the sofa inside. Sal went into the kitchen and brought back a glass of water. When she'd taken a drink, she explained in a near-breathless voice.

"It was an a-ankou. I saw an ankou."

Carissa felt the hair on her neck rise. Alden should have known better than to hang around Vale. She'd told him several times that he could join them in human form, but not to lurk in the shadows. If she admitted outright to knowing the ankou, Hela would spread his identity all over Vale. There were already whispers around Moss Hill that Alden was alive. He wasn't, technically. No one had yet pieced together that he was the ankou, but his state of being was thrown into question when he'd helped his sister fight off the changelings back in February.

"Where?" Raven asked.

"Just down the lane."

"Well, then, let's go. I've been wanting to speak with him. Unless you've already seen him, Carissa?"

"Why would Carissa—" Hela began.

Macara, who also knew the ankou's identity, stood. "Let's go, Raven. Hela, if we see the ankou, we'll make sure he stays away from you and your family. Rest assured."

Maren began, "But Carissa can just call the an—"

"Hela needs to recover," Macara said more sternly.

"We'll come with you," Barnaby said.

He grabbed Holly's shawl and his hat from the sofa chair and wrapped it around her. Practically pushing her out the door, he waved back to the others with a "good night." Carissa didn't blame him. As scared as the fae were of ankous, they trusted the Tuatha de Danann to protect them.

She was a little surprised Hela didn't insist on going with them. In fact, Sal almost began suggesting that they leave together, but Hela put a hand to hear forehead and moaned.

"Goodness sakes, it's just an ankou. You'll be fine," Raven said, pulling the door shut.

Hela's eyes filled with tears. "It was awful. Carissa, Maren, if you'd seen it, you'd be terrified, too. It was a horrible skeleton!"

Carissa sat down beside Hela. "Maybe you saw the trees moving. It's very dark outside."

"And windy, too," Maren added.

Hela raised her voice, "No, it was the ankou."

"You must calm down, dear. It'll upset the baby," Fen said.

Hela ignored him. "He was tall and he was wearing a long, silver cloak. I think he saw me, but he pulled his hood on quickly and turned the corner."

Varick raised an eyebrow.

"Are you sure it was a silver cloak?"

Now that Carissa had read more in her grandfather's books, she also understood the implication.

"It wasn't a coat or something?" Carissa asked.

"No, it was definitely a cloak. Why? Is that important?"

"No," Carissa said too quickly. "Just interesting, that's all."

She looked at Varick. If he knew what she did, he would realize it wasn't Alden outside. The long cloak of the world beyond was a signature of an ankou, though Alden didn't choose to always wear his. But the silver cloak—that was not a regular ankou. That was the reaper of all souls lost in the oceans of the world. It was arguably the most powerful of all ankous: the Ocean Reaper.

"I'll take a look." Varick grabbed his coat from the hooks beside the front door and walked into the night.

"Take care!" Hela called.

"He'll be fine," Carissa's father assured her.

"Why don't I fix you some tea? It'll calm your nerves, dear," Carissa's mother tried to change the topic.

"Shouldn't he take some guards with him?" Hela asked.

Carissa stood. "Cam and I will make sure Varick is all right."

"A human and a half-elf against an ankou?" Hela asked.

"We should be going anyway," Maren said. "We'll help, too."

Maren gave Reg a look. He raised an eyebrow. Opening and closing his mouth, he paused and then said, "Oh, yes, right, no worries. I have some of MacLir's magic, too, so I may be able to help."

Carissa hugged her parents goodbye. Then, all four of them left the home.

"What are we doing?" Reginald asked, stepping through the door and slipping on his coat at the same time.

"Trying to find Alden, right?" Maren asked.

"He's not out here," Varick said, coming back toward the cottage.

"He's not Alden," Carissa added. She explained her suspicions about the Ocean Reaper.

"So, what do we do now?" Reginald asked.

"I'll escort Hela home," Varick said.

"We should leave, too," Maren insisted. "If it's not Alden, I don't want to know what's out here with us."

Chapter 11

Panic Attacks

The bell above the door of the Seelie Tree Apothecary shop rang so many times Monday morning that Carissa's ears tuned them out. The fae of Vale were stocking up on magical supplies. It kept Carissa and Maren both on their toes in the Otherworld.

A tree-dwelling female dryad, whose splintery skin kept the other fae a few feet away at all times, stopped Maren to ask, "What wards off humans?"

Carissa excused herself from assisting a leprechaun buying good luck charms at the register. She raced past the counter before Maren could give an all-too-human reaction. She made it in front of the fae just as her assistant's arms crossed and a snarky reply shot out of Maren's mouth.

"I think you already know how to ward off humans well enough."

Maren disappeared the next second. The human realm would help her cool off, Carissa hoped. She took Maren's place.

"Why don't I show you some ingredients for invisibility spells?" The dryad, scratching the splintery skin of her forehead, followed Carissa down the row.

A morning spent appeasing frightened faeries and pacifying an increasingly offended human dragged on like an eternity. Maren had had enough by quarter to twelve. She marched to the door and switched the sign to closed.

"Maren, we still have fifteen minutes till lunch."

"I don't care. I'm closing."

The click of the latch prompted Carissa to stride to the door. She turned the lock back. Her index finger shot up as Maren eyed the doorknob.

"For goodness sakes, there's still a gnome in aisle three."

Maren rubbed her temples. "I can't take it. It's never been like this before!"

"They're just scared. They've never had humans make it into Vale before."

"And what am I?"

"I mean tourists, Maren. You know that."

Maren let out a banshee-like wail before composing herself to speak again.

"I know. It's just frustrating to hear things like: 'How do you get rid of humans? What scares humans away? As a human, which of these smells are most likely to turn you away from an area?'"

Maren's mimicking raised in pitch until she did a nasally impression of the fae customers.

Carissa said, "I've convinced a few of them to come to the town hall tonight for the Mayoral Meet and Greet. I'm sure Cameron will be able to put their minds at ease."

She put an arm around her friend and walked her back to the counter.

"I hope so. I don't think I can take much more of this."

"More of what?"

A voice behind them provoked a high-pitched squeal from Maren. Her breath hitched as they both spun around. Carissa recognized the speaker even before she saw her.

"What can I do for you, Holly?"

Before Holly could say a word, Maren stomped to the back counter. "Oh, don't you start, too. You can't get rid of humans. We're not pests."

"That's debatable, dear." Holly followed her and dragged a screeching stool to sit at the counter. She looked at Carissa.

"Varick is refusing to care about catching the kidnappers. He's more interested in fortifying Vale like a garrison. He says they're long gone by now, but I know, *I just know,* they're still on this island."

"How do you know that?" Carissa leaned on the counter from the customer side.

"Barnaby saw the woman yesterday—I know you don't believe it. I have a feeling about it, Carissa. They're still out there."

"I don't know what I can do about it. I wouldn't even recognize them if I did see them."

"Ah, see, I've taken the liberty of hiring an artist to draw a picture of her."

Holly fished around in her bag and took out a folded piece of paper. She handed it to Carissa, who opened it to reveal a child's drawing of a blonde-haired, green-eyed woman with a sharp nose and a man with burly biceps, hairy arms, and chest— exactly as Tabitha had described them. They were standing in a forest with a creek and shrubs that produced little berries, some black, some purple, and some red. The leaves were big and the berries disproportionately small.

"It's a little crude, I admit, but Timmy worked for pie and it's a steal for the quality."

"Let me see."

Maren, smiling for the first time today, reached out for the picture. She was perfectly able to walk to them, but Maren stayed put on the chair. Carissa and Holly obliged her.

"Aren't you going to offer an old bean tighe a chair?"

"Sure. There's one in the back room," Maren said.

"Maren," Carissa chided.

Maren rolled her eyes and stood. Holly hopped onto the seat. Carissa handed Maren the note. Then she noticed that her phone had lit up on the counter.

There were several missed messages highlighted on the screen. She picked it up. Two texts and one missed call, all from Tilly Brier.

The reporter had written:

Major info on P & B. Can you meet?

Need your help—can you get away from the shop?

Carissa wrote back, *I'll be at the library at noon.*

"This is very good for an eight-year-old. But what are these?" Maren pointed to the little symbols on the people's clothes.

Holly flattened the image on the counter and tapped where Maren had pointed. "That's an F, and that's an H. Barnaby gave them nicknames. Fish Breath and Honey – a name I'm not crazy about."

"Why did he give them those names? Oh, let me guess, the man smelled like fish?" Maren asked.

"And the woman smelled like honey. At least, that better have been his reason for calling her that."

Maren held the picture up to the light. The shadows behind the drawing changed. The familiar *ding* of the bell announced the arrival of the last customers of the morning.

Warren held the door for Jane, who removed her hat and sunglasses and placed them into her navy handbag. Her blue and white striped shirt was her first attempt at a layperson's outfit, but she still didn't look like a regular Mossie. It was a polite expression to say that a person would look good in whatever they wore. In Jane's case, it was true.

With a determined gait, Jane strode to the counter. Warren followed her lead. His black outfit hadn't changed. Did he only own one pair of clothes?

Maren set the picture down and fussed with her clothes and hair. Her lips tugged down in a sideways slant. Finally, her shoulders slumped. Comparing oneself with a twenty-three-year-old was never healthy for a woman in her thirties, but it was especially disastrous to compare oneself with a beauty like Jane. Carissa wanted to turn to her and say, "*Stop it, you're just as beautiful in your own way,*" but she couldn't say it in a low enough voice for Jane not to hear as she came closer to the counter.

"Carissa, I'm glad you were still open," Jane said.

"Good to see you, Jane. Are you going somewhere special?" Carissa asked.

"Warren and I are investigating an attack in Vale."

"Murder?"

"Jane saw it happen. I was too late to be of any help." Regret drew Warren's eyes down as he looked at Jane.

"It's all right, we were able to save him." She gave a comforting smile.

"We?" Carissa asked.

"Macara and I were just going to Vale when we heard a shout. We ran but, by the time we arrived all we saw was a silvery figure running away. Thankfully, the captain was still alive. Macara is healing him."

"Silvery?" Maren's mouth dropped open. "Does that mean…"

"The Ocean Reaper," Carissa said.

"Who?" Jane needed an explanation.

While Maren provided it, Carissa wondered whether the Ocean Reaper was there to collect the captain's soul after his death or if he'd been the cause of his untimely passing. Why would he be on land at all? And if it wasn't the Ocean Reaper, then who had attacked the captain?

"It was those humans. No one listens to leprechauns. Barnaby warned you about this," Holly said.

"Varick doesn't want to panic the town. We don't know yet whether it was those humans or someone else that injured him, which has put the village into even more unrest than before. Varick's main priority is calming the people at the moment."

"It might calm them more if you caught those kidnappers," Holly said.

Jane said, "Well, that's in part why we're here. Raven asked me to investigate."

"The town or O'Mally's death?"

"Both. I did listen to what Raven had to say and you're right: I'm not convinced it was an accident after all."

"Raven told us the changeling magic we sensed wasn't the woman's own power, it was on the body, as if someone had put a changeling spell on her," Warren said.

"What does that mean?" Maren asked.

Carissa answered. "It means the woman wasn't O'Mally. Someone enchanted her to appear to be the changeling prisoner when she was really someone else. Is that right?"

"We won't know for sure until we look at the body again."

"Take Raven with you when you do go back to the marina," Carissa said.

"Why would they do that? Waste of time, if you ask me," Holly said.

"Raven is too busy today making preparations," Jane answered.

"For what?" Carissa asked.

Jane shrugged. "She and Macara won't tell me. Not yet, they said."

"Is there a reason we should take Raven?" Warren asked.

"She saw through the mayor's changeling magic and could see he was a troll right away," Carissa explained.

"Oh, I see," Maren said. "If Raven can see through the magic, she would know what the woman really looks like."

"I can't guarantee it will work, but with Raven in Vale, we'll have to try druidic magic to see if we can break the changeling spell ourselves," Warren said.

"I have adder stones if you need them," Carissa wondered why she hadn't thought of it before.

Warren put a hand up, "It'll be just as easy. All I need is sumac, sage, apple, thyme, saffron, and some grains of paradise."

"A few of those are rare spices, I think we may have them. Maren?"

Maren's eyebrows flicked in a *why me?* face. Then, they dropped as she must have realized she was the assistant, after all. She trudged her feet around the counter.

"When you're out there, keep an eye out for those kidnappers. Show them the picture," Holly said.

Maren still had the drawing, so she gave it to Jane directly before leaving the conversation. Jane opened the paper and held it between her and Warren. He raised an eyebrow. She smiled. Then, she folded it and handed it back.

"We'll keep this in mind. We were hoping you'd go with us to Vale and then to the marina," Jane said.

"I can't," Carissa told Jane. "Maren and I have an errand to run at lunch."

"Oh, yeah." Maren looked at her watch. "We're going to be late."

She dashed to the back room for their purses.

"If I can close up early today, I'll try to be at the marina this afternoon," Carissa told them.

"Thank you," Jane said earnestly.

Carissa could see her smile falter. Jane seemed relieved. Despite her powerful druid magic, she was as unconfident in her role as Carissa had felt months ago.

The bell above the door rang as Jane and Warren left. Carissa's phone vibrated at the same time. She picked it up.

See you at the library, Tilly's text read.

"I could go with Reg myself if you wanted to go with them to Vale. I know how you like to rush in to examine a crime," Maren said.

Carissa raised an eyebrow. Since when had that become true? She shrugged off the question and showed Maren her phone.

"No, I'll go with you. Tilly's going to join us."

Maren read the texts.

"P & B? What is that, peanut butter and jelly?"

"That's PB & J, dear," Holly said, straining to see past Maren's elbow from her seat.

"It's Parker and Belkin. At least, I think it is. If Parker is up to something regarding the campaign, I have to check it out."

Carissa turned to Holly, who looked like she already knew the question and had her answer ready to fire out of her mouth. She used her most appreciative voice.

"Maren and I might be late getting back. Do you think you could watch the shop?"

"I think you know my condition."

"We'll keep an eye out for the kidnappers," Carissa said.

"Don't just keep an eye out—catch them. Or I fear they'll strike again."

Carissa took her purse and light blue jacket from Maren. They jumped back when they heard a thud behind them at the counter. Two bags, one of dried tansy flowers and one of poppy seeds, landed next to Maren seemingly out of nowhere. Carissa, Maren, and Holly bent to look over the counter. They'd forgotten the gnome who was still in the shop.

"Just those, please," the customer in the pointy red hat said.

"He's all yours." Maren left Holly and walked fast enough for Carissa to rush to catch up.

***

CARISSA AND MAREN met Reg at the information counter. The attendant took them to the reference section where they found Tilly at the back of the stacks. She had her mauve trench coat draped over a chair and a pile of books and notes testing the weight of the table.

"What's all this?" Carissa asked.

Greer's voice called from the other side of the shelf.

"That's all there is. I've told you the book isn't here."

He appeared around the corner with an empty crate.

"Oh, you've called on others to help you. Take as long as you'd like."

"Thanks. We'll put these back as soon as we're done."

Greer held up a hand. "Leave them. I've been meaning to clean out that section since the mayor requested it be updated."

"Cameron made that request?" Carissa asked.

"No, I meant Belkin, sorry," Greer said.

With that, he disappeared around a shelf.

Maren sat down. *"Relics of the Lost Arts,"* she read the book in front of her aloud.

"That's the spine, but it's not the book," Tilly explained.

"What do you mean?"

She handed Carissa one of the texts. Sitting beside the reporter, Carissa read the title page.

"Spells and Incantations of the Druid Order of..." Carissa shook her head. "I can't make out the last word."

"These books look like they're a hundred years old," Maren said.

"Look inside," Tilly encouraged.

"Zen meditation?"

"It's a different book," Maren said. She grabbed another. "They all are."

"No, not all," Carissa said.

The next book she picked up was, in fact, a book on magic and medicinal herbs, but it was old and pages were stuck inside as if they'd fallen out. She flipped through it gingerly. Halfway through, she realized not all the pages were from the same text.

"The ones with dust jackets have a whole new book inside them, and the ones without a jacket have pages that are either missing or have been replaced."

"But why?" Maren asked.

"The question is why these books?" Tilly said.

Carissa could see the pattern right away. "They're all either books on Moss Hill's history or on magic."

"They're the ones I was using in my research. But they weren't like this when I was using them. Someone must have switched them out," Reg said, sitting beside Maren.

"And," Tilly added, "the books that replaced them came from the reference section."

To prove her point, Tilly stood up and took out an identical copy of one of the books stuck inside a dust jacket. She started placing the books back in the crate as she explained.

"Yesterday after the fair, I heard Parker talking with the Belkin about a book and some notes he wanted to get back. He wasn't sure, but he thought the mayor took some items from the library and confiscated them. He thought Belkin may have used his official capacity as mayor to keep the items that Parker had donated."

"A book Parker donated?"

"Fae Secret something…"

"*Secrets of the Fae People?*" Maren ventured.

Tilly's eyes lit up. "Yes! You know it?"

Reg pushed his glasses back from the rim. "Parker didn't donate it. It's mine. I—"

"Gave it to Greer for safekeeping," Maren finished his sentence and stood up. "I should go ask Greer about it."

Tilly held up a hand. "Don't bother. I asked Greer about it already. I didn't know the title, but he said anything on fae magic would be in these archives. The mayor requested to have the section organized in January.

"Parker admitted in December that he'd been looking up information on magic. He said the spells he'd used to create the bad luck charm for the mayor were taken from public information in the Moss Hill Archives," Carissa said.

"There are some spells in the online archive but, based on the titles of some of these books, that's nothing like what they have here, or *had* here," Tilly said.

Reg put his hand to his forehead much like he'd done last night. Carissa didn't need to ask what was wrong. He moaned and looked between the three of women.

"Greer told me when I started my research that no one even realized these books were here until the renovations. They were sitting in the reference section office in the old stacks downstairs. The first time he'd brought them out was for my research."

"And?" Carissa asked.

Reg took a breath before answering.

"I was so excited, I may have been talking about them to anyone who would listen."

"That included Parker?"

"It may have. I talked with Greer about it a few times right here in the reference section. I wasn't exactly speaking in hushed tones either."

"So that means anyone could have switched out these books for fake ones."

"Maybe Parker thinks it was Belkin," Maren suggested.

"He seems to think the old mayor has at least one of the books," Tilly said.

"My book," Reg said.

Tilly added, "There was someone else, a woman visiting Moss Hill who requested that particular text recently—Greer allowed her to check out the book because she was with the publisher. If it was returned, it would be with these."

"Maybe it's not Belkin or Parker, then. My book didn't have the type of spell Parker used in December.

It was mostly spells about seeing fae and revealing powers and…." He turned red.

"Ancient spells. Greer wasn't supposed to let anyone see it. Some of those spells were—" Reg's phone beeped. Interrupted, he excused himself and clicked through the phone as Maren leaned to see what he was writing.

"Sam?"

"Sam Haley, my agent," he answered.

Three curious Mossies would not let him finish typing a response to his text without asking him more.

"Did she say why she published the book without your permission?" Carissa asked.

Reg clicked the send and waited for a response, "She didn't respond when I called before. Now, she says she can't tell me her reasons unless I meet her in Vale tonight. I just told her Vale isn't the best idea."

His phone beeped again. This time he read the text aloud, "'*Vale. 9pm. I'm going with or without you.*' Wonderful," he said sarcastically. "I'm going to have to go and warn her."

"You were saying about the book?" Tilly asked.

Reg breathed deep.

"I'm not proud of it, but I did include some spells about how to steal or transfer fae powers."

Maren paled. Tilly picked up her coat and started putting it on. Carissa voiced the fear in all of their minds.

"So that's why Parker wants the book. If he can steal fae powers, who knows what he might do?"

"We need to get the book back, or at least expose Belkin for having it in his possession," Tilly said as she tied the belt on her thin trench coat.

"What are we going to do? We can't just steal it," Maren said.

"I won't steal, I'll *investigate*." Tilly said it like it was a code word.

"I'm coming with you," Carissa insisted.

"Me too," Maren said.

"If either of you go, our mayoral campaigns are in jeopardy. If you have suspicions, it's best to get a warrant and send in a search," Reg suggested.

"So that they can get rid of the book or have a chance to hide it? Not going to happen. Mossies need to know," Tilly argued.

"Maren, have lunch with Reg and head back to the Seelie Tree. I'll meet you there in about an hour."

Reg shook his head. "You'll get caught."

"You heard Tilly. We aren't going to steal. We'll *investigate*."

Chapter 12

Sylphs and Unseelie

"*Cameron, just letting you know that I have something I need to do with Tilly. I'll be at the Mistletoe estates. I might be near Belkin's, but don't worry, I won't do anything reckless. I'll call you when I'm done. I love you!*"

Carissa hung up the phone with a sudden feeling of nail-biting nervousness. Was this *too reckless?* Maybe it would be if she didn't have a plan the moment Tilly suggested breaking into Belkin's house.

Tilly put her press badge on, reassuring her before they left her car, "It's not breaking in if we're invited into house and ask questions of the staff. If you happen to stumble upon something you know doesn't belong to the mayor, well, that's just a happy coincidence."

"I can't go inside with you. I'm a mayoral candidate's girlfriend. It wouldn't look right."

"So, why did you come with me?"

"I have a friend who can help me sneak in unseen."

"Great, let's talk to him."

Carissa shook her head quickly. "No, I, uh, I have to do it alone. But if you're distracting the butler, I should be able to get in and out before you're done."

Tilly put up her hands. "Enough said. I won't ask you to tell me anymore. Anything he has is probably in his study. Find it. Then, call my cell and we'll be out of there before anyone is the wiser."

"It's a deal."

Carissa almost put a hand out to shake but Tilly was already getting out of the car. Carissa let her fingers fall onto the seat. A handshake would have probably been too much anyway.

Then, she took out the summoning powder from the black velvet pull string pouch she kept with her. Now that Chaos wasn't around to summon Alden, she had to make sure she could do it herself. With a pinch of the powder, Carissa used her elf-light to call on the ankou.

While she waited, she watched Tilly go up the massive steps to Belkin's mansion. Carissa hadn't realized that the former mayor lived in the most expensive neighborhood on the island. It made sense, though. She realized she was falling back on the old notion that trolls acquire masses of wealth, but in Belkin's case, the stereotype might actually fit.

The sides of the stairway were lined with flowers, and a gargoyle sat on either side, giving the place a gothic feel. One of the double arching doors crept open, and a middle-aged man in brown dress pants, a formal white shirt, and a tan vest appeared at the entrance. Tilly began to speak. Carissa cracked the window open so her elf-ears could pick up on the conversation.

"...not here, and I have no knowledge of such an appointment."

As if she hadn't expected this all along, Tilly replied, "He specifically told me today that he would meet me here at this time for a pre-interview. If he's running late that's one thing, but if he's completely forgotten that he talked to me yesterday that doesn't bode well for a person who wants to keep running the whole town."

Carissa chuckled. She was good. Good enough to get in, it turned out.

The moment they left, someone in the back seat whispered, "What are we doing here?"

For the first time, probably ever, Carissa did not jump.

Tilting her head toward the home while glancing sideways at Alden, she said, "I need you to get me in there."

"Belkin's home?"

"You know it?"

"My parents were supporters of Belkin. I've been there before."

Of course, they would have gone to fundraisers and other events the mayor had hosted. Even better.

"Then you must know where the study is?" Carissa asked.

Alden's eyes searched the windows.

"My father would know, but I was never invited to the study before. I'll take us to the entrance. There's a staircase right by the front door and the living room is off center, so if anyone is in there, they shouldn't be able to see up."

Carissa nodded. "As far as I know, Belkin lives alone, and Tilly has the butler distracted."

The unspoken logic was that they should be able to snoop undetected. Alden looked at her curiously. She twisted in her seat to face him.

"What?"

"You know that ankou's powers are not for personal gain?"

Carissa looked away. This wasn't for personal gain. Wrong was wrong. If Belkin was doing wrong, he needed to be caught. If Cameron just so happened to benefit from that, that was a fortunate coincidence.

She sighed. She was beginning to think like Tilly. Facing Alden again, she said, "Belkin may be using a book of spells to try to fix the elections. Parker might be trying to blackmail him to get those spells from him. I don't want to accuse either of them if I'm wrong, but I have to know. This is the best way to investigate."

Alden tilted his head and studied her face. She tried to show her sincerity by keeping her eyes fixed on him. Whatever he needed to see, he must have seen it, because he lowered his chin.

"Switch to the Otherworld," he said as he reached out.

She turned her locket and the world changed to the subtler dream-like tones of the Otherworld. She uttered an incantation to allow her to see into both human and fae realms at once. Then, breathing in deep, she took his hand.

"Hold on. This may feel strange," Alden warned.

"Thank you," Carissa said.

Alden didn't seem to do anything. There was no flick of a hand, no incantation, no ankou magic that she could see. But the world took on a strange quality, almost like a dream—no, not a dream. She was conscious, fully aware, maybe more aware than in either the human or fae realms. It was like pressing one's nose to the outside of a fish tank. Everything inside the world seemed protected in a bubble.

Then the bubble burst and she felt a rush of air, as if she had passed through a portal. He grabbed her shoulders to steady her. She looked up at his black eyes, which were quickly changing to blue.

"I'm all right," she managed to say.

Inside, the home screamed bachelor pad. Everything was brown, from the fur skin rug to the antler-shaped chandelier. Belkin didn't have a reputation as a hunter, so Carissa was sure these were won with money rather than a hunter's skill.

"May I offer you something to drink? Iced tea perhaps?" Carissa could hear the butler before she saw him ushering Tilly to the sofa in front of the fireplace.

Tilly responded that she would love some and he turned to retrieve it. The moment he left, Tilly dropped her convincing fake smile. She made her way to a credenza on the opposite side of the room. Opening drawers and cupboards did not seem to reveal anything before footsteps could be heard again, though the steps creaked from upstairs.

Tilly looked up toward the staircase near the entrance. She did not have time to investigate before the butler returned. Carissa and Alden started for the steps, but halfway up, shadows moved in the hallway at the top of the stairs. Alden put a hand out to keep Carissa back. While they waited for the shadows to move, she could hear the conversation in the living room below.

"Twelve years, Miss."

"And is he a fair employer?"

"The best, Miss. He is very kind to those who are kind to him."

"And those he cares for?"

"Your point?" The butler's tone lit close to his fuse.

"I've heard he was close with the late Tamsin O'Mally."

Tilly's tone wasn't enough to completely douse the spark of anger, but the butler did not explode. Though annoyed, his voice was steady as he answered.

"They were friends, but if you're implying something more, you should know Tamsin O'Mally was married."

Tilly said, "Widowed for at least a year, from what I've learned, and Sean Belkin had a soft spot for—"

A woman's shrill voice pierced the air from above.

"Help!"

Carissa and Alden raced upstairs. It sounded like a struggle, but it was coming from the other side of the home. Alden stopped and turned toward Carissa. He didn't have to say anything. She grabbed his hand.

Alden shifted them into a room that must have been the study. There seemed to be no one there— just papers strewn across the desk and scattered over the floor. Carissa thought they'd found the wrong room, until the scream came again.

"I can't hang on!"

Carissa and Alden hastened to the ledge. A woman's hands clung to the windowsill. Carissa thought she saw something in the sky, but the woman hanging from the ledge took first priority.

"I'm going to have to shift to the human world to save her," Alden said.

"No, wait!"

Footsteps were racing up the stairs. Carissa grabbed Alden's arm and pulled him in front of the desk. If he'd shifted, Tilly would have crashed into him. She and the butler burst through the double doors and right up to the window pane. In the Otherworld, Carissa and Alden remained invisible.

The woman called out again. She was barely hanging on to the window pane. Tilly cursed under her breath and ran to the large, open window.

"Take my hand!" Tilly reached out.

The woman panted as she climbed back up using the offered arms as leverage. Carissa recognized her now: Morgan Jones. The snooping reporter sat at the desk chair to catch her breath, but the butler wasn't having it.

He loomed over her. "Explain yourself."

Between breaths she managed to reply, "I…I was attacked."

"By whom?" Tilly asked.

"You can tell the police. Downstairs, now," the butler gestured for her to move.

Miss Jones flinched as if he were grabbing her, though he never actually laid a hand on her. She pulled away and walked in front of him with her head held high, as if the butler was the one who had committed an offense.

"I'll call the police," Tilly said.

She made for the telephone on the desk. The butler glanced at her suspiciously but, having no real cause to suspect her of anything, followed the intruder down the steps.

Instead of calling the police, Tilly made for the papers. When Carissa and Alden shifted, Tilly jumped back. Carissa put her palms up.

"It's all right—he's with me."

"Did you?" Tilly looked at the window and left the question unasked.

"No," Carissa heard Alden say, but she was focused on the window.

"Do the clouds look wrong to you?" Carissa asked.

Alden and Tilly looked with her.

"It's a sylph," Alden said.

He was right. Carissa had never seen one before. She'd read about them in her grandfather's books, heard stories from Nan, but had never seen one. Yet here it was, clear as day.

Ordinarily, sylphs were like wisps of white that blended in with the clouds. Only occasionally would its face or form be made out against the backdrop of the sky. Now, though, the entire form of the sylph was visible—a humanlike shape making a getaway so fast it left a blurry trail of white behind it.

Almost without thinking, Carissa reached upward. First her elf-light in a bright yellow haze, then her Tuatha de Danann in pink mist shot out of her hands. But Alden pushed her wrist down. Fortunately, she was unpracticed in both kinds of magic and startled enough that the blast dissipated into a fizz of smoke in the air. The faerie flew out of sight.

"The sylphs are elementals. They are never unseelie. If one pushed that woman out of this window, she was doing something it found threatening."

"Maybe she overheard Parker, too. Come look at these," Tilly said.

"*Spells of Fortune, Incantations of Protection, Faerie Sight,* these are the missing books and papers from the library," Carissa said.

"Jackpot," Tilly replied. She held up a slip of paper that had fallen onto the floor. "*Potion of Prestige,* the entire recipe with Belkin's writing on it."

"What does it say?"

"Six p.m., April 22, City Hall."

"That's tonight's meet and greet," Carissa said.

"I'll bet he's planning to use it on the voters in attendance."

"Let me see that." Carissa skimmed the list before handing it back to Tilly, who pocketed it as evidence. "It looks like the potion would be undetectable in water. He could put it in any drink and it would go unnoticed. I can make a potion of my own to reveal the magic. It'll be harmless, but it will interact with the ingredients to show that it's magic. I'll just grab a few things from the Seelie Tree and meet you at the event tonight."

Of course, the delay would mean Carissa would run late for meeting Jane and Warren at the marina, but if it meant stopping Belkin from stealing the election from Cam, it was worth it. Carissa just hoped nothing went wrong at the docks like what happened to Mrs. Jones at Belkin's house.

Unless Mrs. Jones was the one they'd been looking for all this time.

Chapter 13

Parker's Proposition

Carissa met Maren for the end of lunch, ordering a quick smoothie before Reg dropped her and Maren back at the apothecary shop. On the ride over, she explained about the notes they'd found at Belkin's and the almost tragic end of Mrs. Jones. She included what she'd seen in the sky.

"You saw a sylph flying overhead and now you think Mrs. Jones is Mrs. O'Mally?" Maren asked.

"She wasn't at Cameron's speech, and then at the marina she suddenly appeared after the body was found."

"A lot of people showed up, though. The boat's siren was loud enough it's a wonder the whole town didn't come out to see what was going on," Maren said.

"But sylphs don't attack innocent people. There's definitely something off about her."

"Didn't you say she received a tipoff from Parker?" Reg asked.

"Yes, but it's a long way from a tipoff to breaking and entering," Carissa answered.

"You and Tilly did go to Belkin's for the same reason," Reg said.

"We didn't sneak in. Okay, *Tilly* didn't sneak in." Carissa opened the car door and she and Maren walked into the apothecary shop.

"Where is she now?" Maren asked.

"The police have her in custody."

Reg rolled down the window and said, "I'm not sure Cameron wants to speak to me, but do you want me to mention that you're safe and that you'll be joining him at the meet and greet? Or should I say you'll be late?"

"No, that's all right. I'll talk to him myself," Carissa said.

"I won't be late," Maren told him as she blew him a kiss goodbye.

A knot scrunched together in Carissa's stomach. With one line, Maren had simultaneously reminded her that Reg was still Cameron's competition for mayor and that, instead of being the supportive girlfriend, She was only adding stress to Cameron's already stressful campaign. Then again, she was doing this for the town, and didn't that help Cameron in the long run? Then again, it was Jane's responsibility to protect Moss Hill now.

"That's a good thing, isn't it?" Maren's question caught Carissa off guard.

"What's a good thing?"

"That Jones is in custody. A sidhe guard can test her for magic to see if she really is O'Mally."

Right, they were back on the topic of Morgan Jones. Carissa had to remind herself to focus as she opened the door to the Seelie Tree Apothecary.

"Yes and no. If she really is just a reporter, testing her for magic will only give her more proof that fae exist in our town. Raven saw what the woman looks like—the one whom O'Mally is impersonating. I'll just gather the ingredients to test the potion and head straight to the marina to get Raven. She'll be able to identify Jones and then we'll know for sure."

As soon as Carissa's attention drifted from the conversation to the inside the shop, she was surprised to see it just as busy as it had been that morning. Maren went to the counter to help Holly with the customer purchases.

"Carissa, thank goodness," Mrs. O'Brien stopped her. "Which of these is most effective to ward off fae magic?"

She held up a box of St. John's wort in one hand and essence of Rowan in the other while following Carissa. In another row, Mr. Burrows argued with Mr. Morely. Carissa could hear them clearly.

"First the changelings and now this."

"And I've heard it will only get worse."

Carissa turned to Mrs. O'Brien.

"What's going on?" she asked.

"Kelpies nearly drowned a man at the marina."

"A man, which man?"

"I don't know, but there was a group of them. Thank goodness it's a school day or there might've been children in the water. Can you imagine? You know what, I'll take both." She stood in line with the others.

At the counter, Holly practically shouted, "No, it will not 'ward off fairies,' and how dare you even ask me that? Everyone, listen! I am not selling another item to protect you against fae folk. You're perfectly safe, so go home."

She came around the corner in a fury, shooing customers out with little zaps of magic from her fingertips. Carissa protested by calling her name, but in vain. Mossies scattered. Mr. Morely stopped at the door to hold it open for others.

"The voters will hear about this at the city council tonight. You can be sure of that!" he said.

"Wait, Mr. Morely, Mrs. O'Brien, Mary, please." Carissa turned around, crossing her arms. "What on earth, Holly?"

"They're in the best town on earth and they're ungrateful," Holly's voice raised as she spoke. It came back down to a mutter as she rambled, "Humans asking me how to get rid of fae, don't even realize what we've done for 'em."

"Why were they so worked up?" Maren asked.

Holly didn't even look up at Maren, saying, "An attack at the marina. Which, if you ask me, was the work of those kidnappers."

"I doubt humans have the ability to call on kelpies," Carissa said.

"Kelpies? The water horses attacked?" Maren asked.

"Wild ones can do that. It's happened before, years ago…they're rarer than sharks, but it's not unheard of," Carissa explained.

"With Reg giving away magical secrets, I don't doubt that humans have the ability to summon a kelpie or any other fae animal. Never trust a human not to misuse magic once they get hold of it," Holly said.

"Now, *I'm* offended," Maren said, but her half-smile gave her away.

She was probably happy to see someone going through what she endured this morning. Carissa felt a headache starting at her temples. Everyone around was either bickering or panicking. And since when had there been so much animosity between the humans and fae?

Rubbing her forehead, Carissa asked, "Do you know anything else about what happened at the dock?"

"Only that a horse-like fae came out of the water, and a man—not a bright one, obviously—got on the horse and was dragged down into the water. Jane saved him with her magic and that was the end of it. Only it sent a flurry of people over here."

"After all the events these last months, I don't blame them," Maren remarked.

"Well, it only shows me that Jane is going to do a fine job as Moss Hill's protector. The people have absolutely nothing to worry about," Holly said.

Carissa bit her lip. She wished she could be so certain, but just as Holly was so sure about her kidnappers being dangerous, Carissa could see why the Mossies were scared of the unseelie fae who had been plaguing the town. It was undeniable that something was happening in Moss Hill. But was it kidnappers taking fae and fae taking humans separately, or was it all connected? Was it all somehow the work of Mrs. O'Mally?

"I'm off." Holly grabbed her pack and walked toward the door.

"You will be back for tomorrow's shift, won't you?" Carissa asked.

"Yes, yes, but I've had quite enough for today." She waved without looking back.

Maren watched her cross the street. "I guess I'll take the rest of the afternoon shift."

Carissa nodded. "Thanks. I'll collect the items for the potion and then go see if Jane and Raven are still at the docks."

Carissa began with the refrigerated herbs. Sorting through the freezer to the west side of the store, Carissa chose the freshest of the sage and rosemary. She made a mental list of the other ingredients all the while wondering how Belkin might plan to use his potion at the meet and greet. Then she heard a tapping on the glass. Curiously, Carissa stepped back and closed the freezer.

Maren appeared right in front of Carissa's face. Without saying a word, she seized her hand and dragged her toward the back of the store. She stopped at the end of the aisle.

"Look," she said.

Following Maren's lead, Carissa craned her head to see around the shelves. There was a man at the counter. He was dark-haired and dressed in a business suit.

"It's Parker. He says he has a deal for us."

"What did you say?"

"Nothing. I have nothing to say to him. I just came and got you."

"Cam won't like this."

"Just tell him off then. But I don't think he'll leave without an argument."

Carissa let out a frustrated sigh. If Cam was dismayed with her going to Belkin's house, he'd be even more upset about her talking to Parker about a deal. It'd be easier if Maren just told him to leave, but she didn't want the confrontation. Carissa could understand that.

"All right, I'll just tell him to go away. You take care of Sal."

She said the incantation to return to the human realm. Parker turned to watch her as she walked around the counter. He smiled.

"I'm glad you agreed to talk with me."

"I didn't. I'm just here to ask you politely to leave."

"It's not terribly polite to send a person away without hearing them out."

"There is no deal you can offer me that I would take, Parker."

"Not even to get information on Barnaby and Holly's kidnappers?"

She paused and tilted her head.

"I know you're as interested in finding the book as I am. And don't pretend not to know which one I mean. I know you were at Belkin's estate less than an hour ago."

"Where I witnessed firsthand what happened to the last person to whom you made the same request."

"Jones was human. You're not."

"Nice to see you care about her brush with death instead of dismissing her as just human."

"Of course I'd feel terrible if she'd died. But she lived."

"Lucky for you."

"Look, I'm not just asking you a favor. This would be a good deal for you too: if you get the book to me,

I can get you enough info to catch the kidnappers," Parker said.

"Because you're in league with them?"

"I overheard something at the marina."

"Or maybe you don't know anything and are just trying to get what you want."

"I'll tell you what. I heard two things at the dock. I'll tell you one before, one after."

"No deal. Even if you heard something, how do I know you won't use the spells to work your own mischief or use the book to expose Moss Hill to the outside world?"

"I'd never do that. But, if you're worried, I'll just take two pages then."

"I'm not giving you magic, Parker."

"Have a heart, Cari."

Carissa's eyes narrowed at the use of her nickname. He put his hands up.

"I'm going into the world alone in less than a week, Carissa. The sidhe have banished me from Moss Hill. A little help is all I'm asking. Just hear me out."

She crossed her arms. She should tell him to get out, but she said nothing. He took it as an opportunity to continue.

"Before I leave, the sidhe require that I take a binding promise never to expose Moss Hill, so you don't have to worry about that. There's a spell of good fortune and an incantation to ward off evil. What harm can I possibly do with those?"

Carissa couldn't think of a way those two spells could hurt, except that it would make him rich. That was all he'd really wanted in Moss Hill, was it worse out in the real world?

"All right, two spells. That's all."

He offered a hand for her to shake. She eyed it warily, hoping she wasn't making a deal with a devil. He dropped it.

"It's fine. I trust you. We don't even have to shake on it. It's a deal either way."

"What do you know about the kidnappers?"

"They were involved in the near-death of Mrs. Jones."

"And the second clue?"

"The spell first."

"Fine. As soon as I have it, I'll meet you."

"I look forward to it."

His smile made her want to cast a spell on him just to smack the smugness out of him. She watched him leave out of the corner of her eye. After the door had closed, Carissa went to the back room and took out the summoning powder. This time she stood with her back against the wall so that she wouldn't be startled when Alden made his appearance. But he didn't show.

There had been times when that had happened before. This time, though, she felt a chill in her bones. Something was wrong.

"Did you tell him to leave?"

A voice came from the doorway. So much for Carissa's plan not to jump. She stared at Maren as her assistant stepped into the room.

"Alden's not answering," Carissa replied.

"So? He's not very reliable with the summoning powder. You said so yourself."

"I don't have a good feeling about this. Alden said he was sensing another ankou in Moss Hill. And what Hela described last night was the Ocean Reaper. When I saw him earlier, he said he was sensing something at the marina, and now a kelpie may have drowned a man there."

"You think he met the Ocean Reaper at the marina? Could he be fighting another ankou?"

"Or losing to one."

"What do we do?" Maren asked.

"Go to the docks."

"Do you think you could help Alden with the other ankou?"

"If not, there's someone out there who can."

"Chaos?" Maren asked.

"Raven," Carissa replied.

Chapter 14

A Page from Reginald's Book

The boats rocked in eerie silence in the empty marina. If she hadn't spoken to Jane, Carissa would have thought the place was completely abandoned. She approached the king's boat hesitantly. An ominous feeling pulled her back.

"The calm before a storm," Raven said.

Carissa felt the wind get knocked out of her. She grabbed the rope of the gangplank and caught her breath.

"Did I frighten you?"

"No," she lied.

Chaos titled her head to look at Carissa, then tugged at Raven's ear.

"I sense it, too," Raven said. "What's wrong, Carissa?"

"Alden, our ankou, he didn't answer when I called on him."

Raven turned her head sideways and eyes down to look at Chaos. The nature faerie nodded. She put her hands out. Her eyes nearly crossed with how confused she looked. She scratched her head.

"You can't summon him either?" Carissa asked. She looked at Raven. "Something's wrong."

"No use jumping to conclusions. Chaos will check it out."

Chaos's head bounced eagerly. With a nod from Raven, Chaos flew to Carissa and patted her shoulder. Then she swiped her hands from her head to her toes and disappeared.

"Is she going to be all right?" Carissa asked, recalling her encounter in the world beyond.

"Of course," Raven waved a hand. "The question is what are you doing here?"

"Jane asked me to join her and Warren. Where are they?"

"I believe Jane set Warren out to dry, or at least that was my advice."

Carissa raised an eyebrow. Did she mean that literally or figuratively? She shook her head.

"That wasn't all. Jane said you think the woman we found was a human magically changed to look like O'Mally?"

"She certainly didn't look like a troll to me."

"What did she look like?" Carissa asked.

"Blonde, tall, thin."

Carissa smiled. That was Morgan Jones.

"Like the reporter asking Cam all those questions after we left the king's ship?"

"Which reporter? All I saw was a crowd of humans."

"You didn't see her?" Carissa bit her lip. It would have been easier if she knew for sure, or if Carissa had been smart enough to snap a picture of Jones for Raven to see. Carissa held her phone up for Raven to read a text from Tilly.

She explained, "There's a woman whom I think might be O'Mally. She was at the police station, but they've already released her. I think she may go to the Mayoral Meet and Greet tonight. Do you think you can come?"

"Politics isn't really my forte, but if it's to catch a criminal, then yes. I'll be there."

Carissa smiled in relief. Once that was set, she turned her attention back to the ship of the King of Sidhe and Elves. She and Raven walked up the gangplank to the upper decks.

Inquiring about Warren, Raven and Carissa found an elf guard who directed them to a cabin. They found Jane in the doorway averting her eyes from Warren as he changed into dry clothes. Carissa caught the sight of his muscled back before turning her own gaze downward. Raven wasn't shy about anything, it seemed.

"Not a scar on you. Have you never seen battle?" she asked.

Having pulled the black shirt over his head, Warren turned around. He straightened to his full height

"Never a battle that I've lost, ma'am."

Raven's lips curled in dissatisfied fashion. She walked out of the room as promptly as she'd come in. Before Carissa had a chance to ask what that was all about, Warren was up and ready.

"I heard about the kelpie. Are you okay?"

"Physically. Just embarrassed, that's all."

"The kelpie came charging at him. We saw him running down the rocks in human form, by the time it knocked Warren off the dock, it was a kelpie."

"It was running toward you?"

"Or away from something as far as I can tell," Warren said.

"There was a sylph. I don't think you saw it, Warren, but I could see it following behind."

"So sylphs and kelpies are attacking? It's a good thing you're so skilled or Moss Hill would be in far more danger," Warren said.

He was talking to Jane, who blushed and replied, "If I had your talent, I'm sure I could do more."

"You've learned this much almost entirely on your own. Imagine what you could do with even more training," he insisted.

"Yes, yes, we get it. Jane, you saved his life, well done. Warren, stop pushing. Macara is never going to let you train her. And we don't have time for whatever romance is blossoming between you two. In which direction did the kelpie go?"

Jane went beet red. Warren's jaw clenched so tight it was clear he was holding his anger back. Carissa couldn't blame them.

Raven didn't seem to notice the effects of her bluntness. She was more abrupt in her off-putting manners than either of her sisters. Jane was an open-hearted person, but she was flustered far more than anything else Carissa had ever seen. Carissa doubted even Miss Morgan would have embarrassed Jane like that.

Warren outpaced Raven as she made her exit from the boat, saying as he went, "He—it—

disappeared into the water after Jane hit it in the shoulder. I didn't follow for obvious reasons."

What obvious reasons? That he couldn't breathe underwater, of course. There were spells for that, but perhaps he didn't know them. Not that Carissa had any clue. Though the books in her grandfather's study might have something on it. Or maybe the book Parker wanted so desperately had information as valuable as that.

"That's too bad," Raven said. "I'll have to come back at night. Fae with foul intentions are more active at night or on cloudy days. Best to have both if it can be arranged. The seas might arrange one themselves soon." She licked a finger and held it to the sky. "No birds. East wind. Yes, a storm is coming."

One already arrived, Carissa thought. Raven was right, though. There was a chill in the air.

"We chased him for a while. For a moment, I thought he went into a boat, but it was empty when we got there."

"A dead end," Warren said, "and nothing on this ship to give us any clues about Mrs. O'Mally's death."

So, they still believed it was Mrs. O'Mally. Carissa was more certain now than ever that the body wasn't hers. O'Mally may have assumed Jones's form.

Jones was a successful reporter. She might have had a boat of her own in the marina. It would be easy enough to check which one was hers—even easier if it was the same one her accomplice, a.k.a. the kelpie, had tried to use to escape. Carissa didn't think it was that far of a leap to assume the kelpie was her accomplice. It had led the sylph away from Jones, even if she was unfortunate enough to be knocked out of a window in the process. A kelpie wouldn't need a boat at all, unless the person he was working for had asked him meet them there.

"Which boat was it?" Carissa and Raven asked at the same time.

A funny, boastful smile curled Raven's lip. She could keep that pride for herself. Carissa wasn't trying to impress anyone.

Warren shook his head. "You're wasting your time. The kelpie wasn't going for a boat. It was just trying to get away."

Jane said, "I can show you," and she took the lead.

It was farther out than Carissa would have liked. Sure enough, though, at the very end of the docks was a cruiser yacht, easily upwards of what Carissa made in a year at the apothecary shop. It contained décor and clothing accessories that definitely belonged to a woman.

At first, nothing about it seemed unusual. Regular clothes hung in a little closet, a small bed was attached to one wall, and some cabinets were built into the boat's side. A small writing desk built into the cabin beside a large, round window drew Carissa's attention.

On the desk lay some stationary that read: *Kelsey & Addington Press*. That wasn't Jones's paper. More curious was a rose gold pen labeled *Haley* and two four leaf clovers. Jane tried the lower right-hand side drawer.

"It's locked," she said.

"Step aside," Raven ordered.

Warren stepped in the way. "This is illegal. We have no warrant, from human or fae authority, to do this."

"Young man, *I* am the authority. Now, step aside," Raven repeated.

Warren reluctantly stepped to the left. With a simple flick of her hand, Raven caused the drawer to slide open. Jane reached inside. She pulled out a book whose title Carissa recognized right away.

"It's Reg's book," Carissa said as Jane turned it over in her hands.

"Kelsey & Addington Press," Jane read from the copyright page.

Carissa put it together. "I think this boat belongs to someone who works for the company that published Reg's book. Someone named Haley."

"A coincidence?" Jane asked.

Raven and Carissa again replied at once, "I think not."

On the way out, Carissa asked Jane if she could see the book. Warren offered his hand to help Jane off the boat. Raven watched Carissa as she flipped through the pages. On the tenth page, she stopped.

"What do you see?" Raven asked.

Carissa held up the book. The corner of the page had been torn. Carissa had no doubt the missing portion would match the paper that had fallen from the victim's hand.

Carissa said, "This is what O'Mally is after, listen to this." She read aloud, "*Power draining spells. Generally requiring a mix of certain types of fae magic, there are various spells allowing one to give, steal, or switch powers with other fae or even humans.*"

Raven took the book. "This is old magic. Involuntary power switching is against the rules of the seelie."

"But people can voluntarily switch powers?" Carissa asked.

She'd never heard of such of thing. If any magic could do it, changeling magic seemed a likely choice. Raven put a hand to her chin.

"Hmm, so O'Mally wishes to exchange magic. But with whom?"

With the kelpie? The sylph? Or a druid?

"The kelpie attacked Warren, could she be after druid magic?"

"Ordinarily, I would say no. But Warren's family is a powerful one. But you're forgetting someone else who may or may not be under attack."

"Alden! Can she exchange magic with an ankou?" Carissa felt her heart racing.

"If one has the right magic, anything is possible."

Chapter 15

Meet and Greet

Town hall filled quickly. Cameron shook hands and chatted with several Mossies while Carissa and Raven looked around the hall for Morgan Jones. Despite her brush with the law earlier in the day, Jones was sure to appear here tonight. Carissa and Raven weaved their way through the people.

"I don't see anyone matching the dead woman from the boat."

Carissa winced at the words "dead woman." Mossies were already staring at Raven, either because they recognized her or because of her faerie tailored dress. With a variety of earthen colors and a bark-like material that covered the chest like an armored bodice, it wasn't clear if she was celebrating or preparing for a war with nature. Tucking strands of red hair into her updo, Carissa hoped her simple lavender spring dress and white purse would lessen the attention Raven's dress was calling to them.

"She's not here yet," Carissa whispered. She glanced a few times in Cameron's direction.

He wore the same grey suit as the last event, this time with a lavender tie to match her dress. She'd forgotten to call him back from earlier, while he'd remembered the last conversation about how they'd coordinate their clothing for the next mayoral event. She should be with him. She couldn't bring Raven close enough to associate with Cameron. Mossies were wary of the fae right now.

Carissa turned to Raven. "I have to join Cam. If you see a woman who looks like the one from the boat, please let me know."

Carissa hadn't meant it to sound like a command, but Raven answered, "At your service," as if it amused her to receive orders.

With Raven wandering away, Carissa joined Cameron in a conversation with Mr. Burrows. They were discussing renovations across town when Carissa locked arms with Cameron's. He smiled at her briefly while Mr. Burrows continued speaking.

"My company has finished with the castle as long as nothing else happens there. And the hotel was done last year. But it needs some repair since the last…incident."

"The report said the damage was mild and the owners had it insured," Cameron replied.

"My point is that with all this damage, it's difficult to keep up with the cue. Mind you, it's steady business, but I'm not just a contractor. I'm a Mossie, Mr. Larke. This is my home and I need some assurance that it will stand for generations more."

The statement drew in any Mossies close enough to hear it. Carissa would be nervous backed into a situation like this, having to think of the perfect thing to say, but Cameron kept cool under this kind of pressure.

He answered, "Just the idea of unseelie fae was something I used to fear—I still can't assure you that we'll never have an encounter again—but I've learned we have allies among the fae and humans of the island that erase any doubt I once had about our safety. Moss Hill will be around for many generations. We have more on our side than you know."

He put a hand over Carissa's arm. She smiled. Cam meant those words. She'd noticed that he had been braver these days. After a perilous encounter with the changelings, he'd come out with a different approach toward the unseelie. His faith in her seemed unshakable. She wished she had the same confidence.

Her eyes drifted to the refreshment table where Belkin was talking with Mr. and Mrs. Everly. With the wealthy patrons in his pocket, he'd have the whole town with him. But Mrs. Everly excused herself and interrupted Mr. Harbridge to speak with Reginald. Perhaps Belkin was not Cam's real competition.

If Belkin wasn't using magic, he'd be no competition at all. She had the tracer potion in her purse. It was up to her now to reveal Belkin's potion in the punch bowl. But how could she get the antidote into the bowl without it looking like she was the one who'd poisoned it? As more and more people entered the hall, soon there would be plenty of people taking drinks.

"Carissa?"

Mr. Burrows was looking at her. What had he asked? She searched her memory. She'd been only half-listening but knew it was something about the attack in Vale.

Carissa muddled through a reply. "Vale is safe in Sidhe Council's hands, and I believe Moss Hill is more than safe in Cameron's hands. I don't think you or I have anything to worry about."

Cameron smiled at her and continued answering questions from Mr. Burrows and the group that had gathered.

"What's she doing here?" Maren asked, loud enough that Carissa's ears picked the sentence up.

Maren, easy to spot in her red, A-line dress, made a beeline for the door. She was stopped by a dark-skinned woman in a formal black dress. Tilly, thankfully, stood blocking Maren's way. If it was Jones Maren had spotted, a confrontation would have been dangerous.

Carissa tried as politely as possible to excuse herself. Cameron caught her fingers. He leaned in to whisper.

"Do you need me?"

Even in the midst of his campaign, he looked at her as if she were his only concern. Carissa smiled and shook her head, reassuring him that she would be back. She kissed his cheek and walked away from the group, who seemed more interested in Cameron's answers to their questions than his moment with his girlfriend. She would never have left Cameron's side if she wasn't doing so for all of Moss Hill.

Carissa made her way to Maren and Tilly, interjecting herself into their conversation. Maren had, in fact, seen Jones. Tilly filled them in on what little she'd learned.

"Jones didn't say anything except to her lawyer, someone from a London firm. All I was able to find out is that they released her because Belkin didn't press charges."

"Why not?" Carissa asked.

Was it because Jones was really Mrs. O'Mally? Carissa knew that Belkin was once engaged to Tamsin. Was he still in love with her?

Maren inhaled like she'd just had a brilliant idea. "You still think she's O'Mally, though, right? Didn't you say Raven could identify her as the person from the ship? I'll go get her."

She walked away before anyone could say anything more. Tilly began to follow. Carissa pulled her back.

Opening her purse, she handed Tilly the vial. Tilly slipped it into her purse. In exchange, she handed Carissa the note with Belkin's writing and the potion's ingredients.

"Reginald suggested I take it to Vale. I think he's right. It is a fae matter, after all. But—"

"But Vale might not be the best place for a human right now. I understand. I can take it there myself," Carissa assured.

"If you find anything else out in Vale about the kidnappers, Belkin, or anything, you'll tell me, right?"

Carissa nodded and Tilly mixed in with the crowd.

Carissa should have immediately gone to find Maren and Raven, but instead she thought about what Tilly had just revealed. A lawyer from London? Carissa knew one person who had pretended to be a lawyer before to get information from Mossies.

Her eyes wandered to Reg, who was now laughing with Mrs. Harbridge. Carissa walked straight to Reg and confronted him. He did a double take as she approached. He asked Mrs. Harbridge if she could excuse him before turning to Carissa with a wide-eyed, nervous smile.

"What?" he asked innocently.

"You're not a lawyer, Reg," Carissa said.

He looked like he might deny it, but then he pulled at his collar while taking a drink. His fidgeting gave him away. Carissa whispered her accusation.

"You knew about Jones being in Belkin's house, and your father owns a law firm in London. There was no way another English lawyer could get to Jones so fast. You went to the police station posing as a lawyer so you could talk to Morgan Jones."

"I didn't tell her I was a lawyer, only that I represented my father's firm and that we could send a lawyer from England if needed. All true."

"You don't know what you've done, Reg. Do you realize who she is?"

"I know who you think she is, but we can't risk it. Unless there's a spell to wipe memories, we have to assume she really is a reporter from London. If she is and she finds out there really are fae on this island, that's the end of Moss Hill."

"It's the end of your campaign if you're helping criminals. If Jones turns out to be O'Mally, you'll be breaking the Mossies' trust in you."

"I think Holly is doing a fine enough job of that." He glanced at Holly, who was chatting away with several Mossies and making sidelong glances in his direction. She was definitely talking about Reg. He set down his glass and put his hands up defensively.

"I only went there to find out more about what happened. But then her being in that jail cell while the officers were all talking about the kelpie attack in the marina—that would only confirm her suspicions about faeries existing on the island. Reporters gathering any kind of evidence about the fae in Moss Hill could hurt Vale and all the fae who live on the island."

"How did you get Belkin to agree to drop the charges?"

Reg tried to appear nonchalant as several Mossies walked by. He lifted the glass to his mouth to cover his words. Smiling through his teeth, he answered in a low voice.

"I got him to agree to more than that. He just announced he's dropping the race a few moments before you arrived. The Everlys are trying to convince him to stay in, but he won't change his mind."

"How did you get him to do that?"

"I told him that we knew about the potion he planned on using for tonight's event. I informed him that the Sidhe Council will be more lenient if he doesn't actually use it."

"You can't guarantee the Sidhe Council will be lenient about anything."

Reg dropped his head, shaking it. "Carissa, I've been trying to tell you and Cameron that I'm not doing any of this by myself. I wouldn't even be in this campaign if it were up to me. I know how much it means to Cameron, but this is what MacLir wants for this town—me here, in charge, as his proxy. I know more about the fae than anyone here. There are things this town is being protected from—even knowledge about its own past and what's in store for its future. MacLir wants someone in office who the fae will listen to when trouble starts."

"What does that mean?"

"I can't say. Not here. But I will tell you that based on what Jones said today, the trouble is already starting."

"What did she say?"

"She was looking for the book as tipped off by Parker when she was attacked by a man who was rather large and very hairy. She wouldn't have gotten away except that a 'cloud person' saved her."

He looked at Carissa, waiting for her to make the connection.

"The sylph and the kelpie. Warren said the kelpie was being chased by a sylph. It must've followed the kelpie from Belkin's home."

Reg added, "If Jones is telling the truth, then the kelpie pushed Jones out of the window. The sylph must've seen it and tried to help her."

"Or," Carissa countered, "Jones and the kelpie were both attacked by the sylph, who saw they were breaking into a home."

"It all depends on whether Jones is really Mrs. O'Mally," Reg said.

Exclamations erupted as a tray clattered to the floor at the far end of the room. A crash and the crunching of glass under heels filled the room as Mossies hurried away in opposite directions. Their scattering revealed Raven Corvus madly dashing to the door.

Carissa ran without thinking. She caught up with Maren and Tilly outside. In the confusion of the dispersing crowd, Carissa could not find Raven.

"What happened?" Carissa asked.

"O'Mally ran the moment she saw Raven," Maren explained.

"There!" Tilly cried.

Carissa spotted Morgan Jones near the bushes by the library. She used her elf-light to speed toward the area. Once she was close enough, she tried to gather enough Tuatha de Danann magic into her hands covertly to catch Jones off guard. Pink mist is hard to miss.

"It's not her!" Maren yelled too late.

Jones turned around, phone in hand. She wasn't running away from Raven. She was running toward her story. And now she had Carissa's magic on tape.

More than that, changeling magic hit Carissa the next second. Her own magic dissipated as she hit the floor. Her purse flew away from her, and in her dizzy state, all she could see was a blonde woman running away.

Jones fainted the next second. Raven stood behind her. Tilly picked up the camera Jones had dropped. Maren helped Carissa up.

"We don't have to worry about the tape," Tilly said, repositioning it in Jones's hands.

"Nor her memory," Raven added. "I'm sure we can convince her she had some kind of nervous episode. Humans believe that, I think."

Carissa, still phased, said, "My purse."

Several Mossies helped pick up the items that had fallen. Tilly handed the bag back to her, slipping the potion inside. It was a good thing the vial was with her or it might have looked incriminating to have a potion in her purse at this kind of event. Carissa looked at Tilly questioningly. The reporter shook her head. Belkin hadn't used it.

Maren gathered the rest of her items from the Mossies and thanked them. Raven told the crowd the event was over. That was that. When the Mossies had all gone, a single piece of paper lay in the street. Raven picked it up and brought it to Carissa. She wasn't yelling but scolded Carissa as she handed her the note.

"If you hadn't interfered, I would've caught that changeling. I—" She stopped.

"What is it?" Carissa asked.

Raven took the partly opened drawing and unfolded it completely.

"Here she is. This is the woman O'Mally is impersonating."

"Holly and Barnaby's kidnappers?" Maren asked.

Realization hit Carissa with more force than the tempest that had brought Raven to Moss Hill.

She shouldn't have been looking for O'Mally, the kelpie, *and* the kidnappers. O'Mally and the kelpie *were* the kidnappers.

Chapter 16

Appearances and Deception

"Parker said the kidnappers were at Belkin's mansion," Carissa explained to Raven, Tilly, and Maren as they stood in the street. "One of them is O'Mally, the other is the kelpie. They're working together."

"I knew it!" a voice came from out of the building. Holly and Barnaby walked toward them. Cameron, Reg, and Belkin were not far behind, as were a few other Mossies.

Holly rambled, "I mean, I didn't know it was O'Mally, but I knew those kidnappers were more powerful than regular humans. They kidnapped a nature faerie!"

"Not to mention us," Barnaby said.

"What happened? Carissa, are you okay?" Cameron asked. He crossed the street in seconds. Reg mirrored the same sentiments with Maren. They both assured them that they were all right.

Raven gathered their attention. "There is a London reporter who needs attending to."

"I'll take care of it," Belkin assured.

"I'd better help you," Reg said, but Belkin walked as briskly as a large-boned man could walk.

"I may not be perfect, but I do care about this town. I can take care of this woman." Belkin looked at Raven for help.

Raven waved to Reg. "Come back, young man. We have other things to discuss."

Carissa began filling Cameron in on the events. He pulled the group back inside City Hall up to his office to finish the wrap up. It ended up with Cameron pacing back and forth. The others sat in various spots in the room, following him with their eyes.

"I don't care if Belkin is hiding a murder confession—you don't break into a house!" Cameron finally said.

"Morgan Jones broke into the house and we wouldn't have realized that the sylph chased the kelpie to shore if we hadn't seen it."

"And if you were the one pushed out the window?"

"I had Alden with me."

She didn't need to explain that few fae would dare attack an ankou. And if she'd been pushed or someone had tried to harm her in any way, she could have escaped with an ankou's ability to instantly travel anywhere. Cameron's fears were unfounded.

"We did find something that helps your campaign," Carissa said.

"Your dying doesn't help my campaign."

Carissa could see the fire in Cameron's eyes almost as if he were a sidhe. Uneasy glances traveled around the room. Cameron didn't miss that, either.

"Am I the last to know this?" he asked.

Carissa cringed. She took the responsibility of answering.

"You were busy with mayoral responsibilities and preparing for tonight's event. I didn't want to add to your stress."

Cameron ran his hand through his hair. Reg stood and put his hand on Cameron's shoulder.

"She's all right. And now we have our suspects."

"The kidnappers," Barnaby said.

"I'm not following. How is Mrs. O'Mally one of the kidnappers? Wasn't she on the boat when Holly and Barnaby were taken?" Maren asked.

"No, it was noon by then. I'd just taken my lunch break," Holly said.

"She must've left the boat with the help of the kelpie, killed a woman at the Marina, and taken her form," Carissa ventured.

"Then she used her changeling magic, brought her back to the ship, and pretended she had fallen off the ledge. Is that your theory?" Tilly asked.

"Wouldn't the body be wet?" Maren asked.

"Not necessarily. Kelpies can run on top of water."

"There was a little water near Mrs. O'Mally's body," Cameron recalled.

"I see," Barnaby's eyes lit up. "So, the kelpie placed the body under the stairs while the real O'Mally ran and hid among the crowd at the marina."

Reg shook his head. "But how did a kelpie have strong enough magic to get her out of her prison?

Both the room and her restraints were layered in elf, sidhe, and druid magic. You'd have to have—"

"An old, ancient, and powerful spell," Raven finished his thought.

"Like the books Parker is after. Looks like I'll have to interview our old friend." Tilly stood up.

"Ancient spells!" Holly's shout captured all of their attention. "Barn, she didn't want our treasure! She wasn't using the nature faerie to weaken us and steal leprechaun treasure. She was draining magic from us. She used the silly tale from Reg's book to make us think she was a brainless human. Oh, no offense."

"Some taken," Maren teased.

"Haley had my updated book. They did get the spells from me, gosh, Holly, Barn, I'm so sorry." Reg said.

Carissa said, "We have to find O'Mally and that kelpie before they have a chance to use whatever spell they're working on."

"If we find them, we might also find our missing people," Raven said.

"What do you mean?" Maren asked.

Carissa stood. "Chaos and Alden. They still haven't returned from the world beyond."

"Yes, they have. I can feel that Chaos is all right, but she's in Vale. Are you with me?" Raven asked Carissa.

She took a step toward Raven.

Cameron stood between them. "Not without me."

"No. No humans. It's too dangerous," Raven said.

Cameron's eyes were pleading. "Carissa, I know you have magic, but you're not indestructible."

"Cameron goes and so do I. I still have some of MacLir's magic, remember? Plus I have to warn Sam," Reg said.

"What about me?" Maren stood.

"You can come with me," Tilly said. "If you want to confront Parker with any unspent hostility, I really wouldn't mind having you along."

Maren's chin quivered, but then she straightened her back and pressed her lips firmly into a smile.

"Deal," she said.

Before Holly and Barnaby asked, Raven gave them their orders.

"Go to Tabitha's. Tell her to be ready. It's always good to have a changeling when you're up against another. As for the three of you, I'll get Jane and Warren and meet you in Vale within thirty minutes No cars. Carissa, you can use your elf-light to speed the journey, but if you take a car to Vale, I'm afraid they'll shoot the tires before you get there."

"I understand, but make it an hour," Carissa said. She turned to Cameron. "Tilly, can you give Maren and me a ride to my house? If I'm going to be useful, I have to change out of this dress first."

"Speak for yourself," Maren said. "If anything, I think I'll be more useful in this."

"What does that mean?" Reg asked.

Cameron stopped what might have become an argument with a clap of his hands.

"We're settled then. Reg and I will change, too, and meet you at your house as soon as we can. Let's go catch these kidnappers."

***

"WE AREN'T REALLY here to just change clothes, are we?" Maren knew Carissa long enough to understand the way her mind worked. She sat on the bed while Carissa changed in her closet. Appearing again in jeans and a green top, Carissa pulled the pins out of her red hair and twisted it into a ponytail.

"No, there's something I need in my grandfather's study."

"Well, hurry up. Your nan makes a great cup of tea, but I don't think she can occupy Tilly for too long. She is a reporter and bound to want to come up here."

"Okay, let's go, but not you two."

Two sneaky nature faeries thought they were slick enough to slide the window open. They were halfway through before Carissa spied Hiya and Cynth.

Hiya began to argue.

Carissa replied, "Everything's fine. No, I don't know where she is, but I'm going to Vale to find her. You and Cynth stay here."

Cynth shook her head and stomped her feet. Carissa gave her an I-mean-it look. Then, she walked to the window to shoo the sprites away.

"Maybe they should come. They have magic, too. It could be a good sneak attack to have them stay behind you," Maren suggested.

"Don't give them any ideas," Carissa said, shutting the window.

They exited into the hall, spriteless, and stood in front of the study. Carissa placed her palm on the door and the whole of it lit. Then, she opened it. Maren had seen the trick so many times she looked at it unimpressively now.

"What is it you need in here?" she asked as they entered.

Carissa walked toward her grandfather's desk and pulled out a drawer. She retrieved a small, black box and turned it around in her hands. Maren walked around the mahogany monstrosity to see what Carissa was holding.

"Here it is," Carissa said as opened the lid.

Maren gasped. "It's beautiful!"

There was a men's Claddagh ring with a white and yellow gold band alternating between the Anam Cara Knot—or celtic love knot—and the claddagh hands holding the heart and crown. She'd recognized it from her family portraits but never seen it in person until she'd found it weeks ago in the desk.

"My grandfather's wedding ring," Carissa said. "Nan and I found it last week. She gave it to me with the only condition being that I give it to someone I love."

"Now might not be the best time to propose," Maren said.

Carissa smiled. Claddagh rings could be worn for many reasons. Much like the one Cameron had given her on Valentine's Day, she would give this one without proposing marriage.

"As much as I would love that, I had something else in mind."

Carissa took the ring out of the box and handed it to Maren. Then, she replaced the box in the drawer and opened one of the books from the nearest shelf. Maren held the ring up to the light to admire it while she waited.

"It doesn't look like a regular band. It's too shiny."

"It's elf-made, infused with magic to fit the wearer."

"Too bad it wasn't charmed to protect your grandfather. It may have saved his life."

"That was my idea exactly."

Carissa set the book on the table. She held her hands out to take the ring. According to the instructions in the book, Carissa closed her eyes and allowed herself to feel everything she felt for Cameron Larke. Mostly, she was overcome with her desire to keep him safe. After a while, she could feel her Tuatha de Danann magic flowing through her.

"Wow," she heard Maren say.

By the time Carissa opened her eyes and looked, the pink glow of her magic was already fading. The ring shown even brighter than before. Slowly, it settled back to a more ordinary, though still radiant, hue.

The doorbell rang downstairs.

"Cam and Reg," Maren said.

Carissa placed the ring in her pocket and walked with Maren out the door.

"I don't want Cameron to know he's under the protection of Tuatha de Danann magic. I'd rather he just think I'm making a romantic gesture in the face of danger."

Maren stopped her at the top of the stairs.

"Speaking of romantic gestures, there's something I should tell you. Valentine's Day, when you thought Cameron might propose, he wasn't really going to ask you about being mayor. I told him you weren't ready for him to ask you to marry him."

"What, why?"

"Because you said you weren't ready! You looked like it anyway. I'm sorry, I shouldn't have given him any advice. I just thought it was what you wanted."

"Carissa? Are you ready?" Cameron called from the base of the stairway.

"You and I will talk about this later," Carissa said.

Once downstairs, Maren left with Tilly. Reg, now in a pair of brown pants it looked like he'd borrowed from Cam, walked her out and said he would start up the car.

Cam's casual attire wasn't how she was used to seeing him, but his muscled frame was more visible in the t-shirt.

He explained, "We'll only take it as far as the castle and walk from there to Vale woods. What's wrong?"

She handed him the silver and gold band. "For luck."

He took it and slipped it onto his right-hand ring finger. Then, to repay her, he pulled her into a kiss. She gave herself completely to the moment, hoping the memory would stay with him through whatever danger they were sure to face next.

Chapter 17

Spring into Action

There was no path into Vale. At least, there wasn't the same one that had been there before. No stairway of stones was visible in either the Otherworld or the human realm. If not for the forest fae, Carissa would not have found it. Though, it seemed their job was to keep the humans out.

"This way."

"No, this way is nicer."

"Fee-Fi-Fo—"

"That's for giants. I already told you we're not doing that!"

It would have been intimidating if Carissa hadn't known that it was not ghostly voices trying to mislead them.

"You know it's me, right?"

She bent over with her hands on her knees, picking out the camouflaged duergars with her eyes. Slowly, one of them rose. Its brown, mud-covered clothing dripped as the little hairy man raised a hand to his chin.

Reginald recognized them. "You're the ones! You threw around my glasses the first time I was here!"

The duergars cackled. The one who Carissa was still looking at finally answered her question.

"How do we know it's you?"

Cameron tapped his foot impatiently. "She sees you all the time."

The duergar crossed his arms. "Then what's my name?"

Carissa shook her head. "You never told me your name."

He stuck his index finger at her nose. "That's right! We never tell."

This roused cheers from the group of "go away, humans!"

Carissa took a page out of Holly's book and zapped the main duergar with some harmless elf-light magic.

"Ow!" He rubbed his hip.

"She's fae," another said casually, confirming to the others that she could now pass."

"Shame on you, all of you. You've always let the humans of Moss Hill visit Vale as long as we knew the way from start to finish."

"The path changed."

"Since when? Oh no, don't answer." She put a hand to her forehead and rubbed. She looked at Cameron and Reg. "Varick has been fortifying Vale. They thought human kidnappers were running amuck."

"Can you show us the new path?" Reg bent down to ask.

The leader leaned forward so that his nose was touching Reg's. An eyebrow raised suspiciously as the duergar spoke accusatorily.

"But how do we know…?"

Carissa had had enough. She picked up the duergar in her hands and looked him in the eye. "I am Carissa Shae, daughter of Dorian and Kaley, half-elf and apothecary of Moss Hill, and if you don't let me pass, I will zap you again."

"Okay, okay, let me go!"

They grumbled their apologies and began running and pointing in a zig zag fashion that was completely unnecessary. It made the trail difficult to travel. It twisted far from the now invisible stairway and steeply up a hill so that the three of them were breathing heavily by the time they reached the top. Such a difficult route did not bode well for most Mossies to visit.

Once at the summit, it took Carissa a minute to get her bearings, even in the Otherworld.

"Where are we?" Reg asked.

The duergars all pointed in the same place and then scattered. They followed where the pint-sized fae hands had directed and looked up. It was the redwood tree. Carissa almost hadn't recognized it as she was viewing it from the opposite side. This was the very edge of Vale. They had gone all the way around it.

"This is ridiculous," she muttered to herself while she trekked through the giant roots gripping the moss-covered ground.

"Halt! Who approaches?"

The booming voice stopped her in her tracks. She matched the volume.

"I am Carissa Shae."

She was near angry enough to demand to speak with Varick at the very least if not the Sidhe Elders themselves. It turned out she didn't have to. Varick was already outside, along with Raven, Jane, and Warren.

"Finally," Raven said.

She began walking too briskly for people who had just run a mile uphill. With her elf-light and Cam's years of playing sports in school, they fared better than Reg, whose loud breathing caused Raven to turn around several times.

"Sorry, where are we going?" he asked almost breathlessly.

Jane said, "Raven thinks they've gone to Tabitha's or near the river there."

They came to a part where the roots of the redwood rose high enough to have to climb over. Varick leapt up and reached a hand down to Jane. She smiled at him and took it. He didn't miss Warren's hand on the small of her back giving her the leverage to clear the wood. Carissa didn't miss the scowl on Varick's face. He helped the others over as well, except for Raven. For the Tuatha de Danann, the ground seemed to continue as if the root was not even there.

"Can't you transport us?" Reg asked.

"We wouldn't have the advantage of a surprise attack. We have to see the land first."

"We could go to Tabitha's," Carissa said, wishing she'd thought of it when they were still on the other side of Vale and closer to where the tylwyth teg lived.

"Not Tabitha's, the kidnappers are just as likely to have taken over the place."

Cameron stopped in his tracks. "You told Holly and Barnaby to go there!"

"See, this is why we're walking. If you're going to shout, we can't surprise anyone."

Cameron walked closer to Raven. Though his voice was quieter, it was no less harsh. "You deliberately sent them into a trap."

Raven seemed unshaken. "I can't sense the changeling's magic unless she's using it. If they try to catch the leprechaun and the bean tighe, I'll be able to trace them."

"You don't know where they are. They could be anywhere in Vale," Reg said.

"Chaos's magic is weaker than I expected," Raven admitted.

Carissa was more worried about what Raven had said about Chaos than about the fact that she had no idea where she was going. Why was the nature faerie's magic weak? Did she mean it was weak in general, or had she lost some power since she'd gone to find Alden?

"Is she hurt?" Carissa asked.

"Possibly," Raven replied.

She didn't take her eyes off the road now that they'd come to Vale.

"You don't care," Carissa realized.

Raven stopped. For a moment, she thought the woman might tell her that she really did care or show some sign of emotion. But, no, she only put a hand up. The group stopped.

"Got them," Raven said. She turned around. "Hold on to each other. This is going to be a dizzying ride."

***

CARISSA MIGHT HAVE said the room was spinning if there was a room, or walls, or anything to orient them in space and time. For the worst seconds of Carissa's life, there was nothing around her. And then there was.

She hit the room with incredible force before she realized she hadn't moved at all. She was just suddenly there. The spinning had stopped. She was inside a house with a bed, a nightstand, a dresser, and a picture frame lined up with a window. The roof was slanted and the walls tilted in the oddest design. It had to be Tabitha's home.

Reg fell to his knees and gagged. Cameron, though disoriented, made a clumsy attempt to help Reg back up. Carissa took a step forward. The room seemed to slant sideways and she found herself falling into a wall.

"The effect will wear off in a minute," Raven said.

Closing her eyes and waiting for her breath to steady, Carissa finally pushed herself away from the wall. Cameron was there to wrap an arm around her. She assured him she was all right. Though, she realized something was wrong.

"Where are Jane, Warren, and Varick?"

Raven shushed her. The Tuatha de Danann walked to the door. Before she opened it, she whispered, "They're protecting the town in case anything goes awry. That's their purpose in being in Vale. Now, keep quiet."

Carissa stepped closer to the door, through which Raven was now peering. Reg and Cameron stood behind her. In the silence that followed, a low din of voices rose from below. Raven looked back at them.

"They're downstairs. You two make your way down there."

"What? Just us?" Reg asked.

"We're the distraction," Cameron realized.

Carissa stepped in. "Wait, no, you already sent Holly and Barnaby—they'll be here any minute."

"They're already here." Raven let out a frustrated breath. "I'm not used to explaining myself. All right, here it is: I can hear them tying up Holly and Barnaby. You two are going to try to catch them by surprise, which probably won't work. I'll appear in the kitchen and attack. Carissa will sneak in and rescue Chaos and the ankou."

"That many people to attack a changeling and a kelpie?" Carissa asked.

"If that's all who's down there," Raven said.

Carissa grabbed Cameron's arm. It wasn't shaking exactly, but she could see him trying to gather his courage as he stepped forward. She reached up and gave him a kiss on the cheek.

"Be careful," she said.

He looked at her with a half-courageous smile.

"I have some Tuatha de Danann magic with me, right?" He looked at Reg. "What could go wrong? Not a real question, please don't tell me."

"Tell me," Reg pleaded. "I've never actually faced a fae before."

"You'll be fine. Use one of MacLir's potions if you need to." Raven moved behind him and pushed both boys out the door.

Carissa wanted to give her a piece of her mind, but she was nervously watching the two try to tiptoe across creaking floorboards and down an old staircase.

"Who's there?" a male voice called from below.

Cameron glanced at Reg and then, as if both had had the same thought, the two rushed forward. Reg made a war cry toward the bottom steps. Carissa winced as she heard a crash. She turned sharply.

"You have to help—"

But Raven was already gone.

Heart racing, Carissa was left alone with the task of finding Alden and Chaos.

She made her way downstairs. A few more rickety steps would not be heard in the fight that was going on. At the last step she came to a distressingly dark hallway. There was a flicker of light a few paces down to the right and another all the way at the end of the hall where a door led outside. She walked along the wall and passed by an opening where she could see Cameron and Warren untying Holly and Barnaby in the living room.

She thanked heaven they were okay.

The next second, they ducked as multicolored sparks came flying from the kitchen. Carissa ran in to help. Cameron caught her arm.

"Raven has it handled. Go find Alden."

"Where is he?" Carissa asked.

Barnaby spit out his gag as Reg took the cloth from his chin. "The hallway. He, Chaos, and Tabitha are in one of the rooms."

Carissa crouched back into the creepy hall. Hurrying to the first door, she opened it to reveal a room of fabrics and looms. Stepping farther in, she could see a cracked sewing machine tilting against a wall.

"Tabitha!" she shouted.

The tylwyth teg lay on the floor in a similar position to the woman on the boat. A fresh cut on her forehead looked like it was still bleeding. To be certain, Carissa dropped to her knees and leaned to press her fingers on Tabitha's neck.

"Please be alive," she whispered.

She was. Barely.

Carissa tried to heal her with elf-light. She'd been learning. Did she know enough yet for this to work? A door swung open and banged against a wall. Carissa flinched. Her elf-light dimmed to nothing as she turned her head.

It wasn't the door to this room. It sounded farther away. The front door, possibly. Was someone entering the house or running away?

"Wha-what's happening?"

Tabitha's eyes moved under their lids as she came back to consciousness. Her hand moved to her forehead. She winced in pain.

Carissa grabbed a cloth from the nearby table. She pressed it against the injury. Taking Tabitha's hand and curving her fingers around the fabric, she managed to get her to press firmly on the cut.

"Stay here. Don't try to sit up. I'll be back as soon as I can," Carissa said.

Sprinting to the hallway, she wondered for a split second again whether she should help the others or stick to finding Alden and Chaos.

"Reg, now!" she heard Cameron yelling.

Despite wanting to help, Carissa told herself that they sounded like they had things under control. She made for the next room. The door was locked. Without even thinking, her Tuatha de Danann magic worked its charms around the frame.

Once inside, she spotted Alden kneeling on the floor before the sun caught her eyes. She held an arm up and blinked. The setting sun coming in through the open window sharply contrasted the dark hall and the curtained windows of the sewing room. Then, she realized.

Open windows?

Her eyes adjusted and she traced the window, which was open just a crack, to the rest of the room. There was a fireplace, a chaise, some chairs tipped over, and a table where a mesh wire birdcage sat open. Inside were three nature faeries. One of whom was being attacked by the others.

"Hiya, Cynth, what are you doing?" Carissa yelled as Hiya lifted Chaos by the collar and slapped her face.

When he heard Carissa call out, he dropped Chaos and turned red. He looked at Carissa sheepishly and started to explain. Carissa was too focused on Chaos to understand his hand signals.

Cynth had taken over and was now on top of Chaos performing some rudimentary chest pumping from CPR scenes she'd no doubt seen on television. Hiya's waving became more sporadic.

"Okay, I get it, you went off searching for Chaos even though I told you not to and you found her just before I came in. Now, let her go. I've got her."

Carissa stepped closer to the cage.

"Carissa?" The sound of Alden weakly calling out her name stopped her.

She watched the nature faeries continuing to try to revive Chaos. Hiya was floating over a plant on the mantle. He sprinkled faerie dust over it.

"Don't," Carissa put up a finger to warn Hiya before turning her attention to Alden.

He called out again, "Cari?"

"I'm here," she said.

Carissa knelt behind him to check the ropes. It was magic like what she'd seen the sidhe use to create a stretcher for the body on the ship. Only this was a pulsing, purple, changeling magic, and it held Alden's wrists and ankles together. Alden's back was straight but his head was down, the hair falling over his eyes.

"Can you use your ankou powers to fade your hands and legs from the rope?"

"Can't, too weak," he strained to say.

Carissa could see how his chest hitched in pain with every other word. Despite her inexperience, she would have to use her Tuatha de Danann powers to try to break the bindings.

She ignored the *splash* that was no doubt Hiya disobeying her order not to throw all the water from the flowering plant onto poor Chaos. Instead, she held the rope.

"*Tuatha de Danann magic is about feeling,*" she recalled what a sidhe guard had once told her. She held her hands over the rope and tried to let a feeling of freedom wash over her. That was the appropriate feeling here, wasn't it?

The only problem was that wasn't what she'd been feeling lately. Finding out she was Tuatha de Danann, Raven telling her she was a protector of Moss Hill only to find out later that the sidhe had other plans, the fear of having to leave Moss Hill, all of these feelings got in the way.

But then, Jane wanted to leave and couldn't. Carissa had the freedom to go anywhere. She would be all right with that, if Cam was there. Anywhere she was, if the man she loved was with her, that would be freedom.

The rope started to loosen. Carissa opened her eyes. It wasn't enough. She could feel power flowing through her, but it wasn't infusing deeply enough into the rope.

She would have to touch the bindings.

It was going to hurt. It might hurt both her and Alden. She took a few short breaths, then she shouted to Alden.

"Hold on."

The instant she touched the chords, magic struck her like weaponized fire. The bindings glowed orange. Carissa and Alden both screamed in pain.

Then, a cooling rush of power flooded the air all around her. With a crackling and sparks of faerie dust, magic brightened to a white light. The rope melted in her hands and disappeared.

Alden fell to his side. Carissa gasped and held onto the table to hold herself up. She looked in the direction of the mantle.

Two smug nature faeries gave each other high fives and shook hands, congratulating each other. Chaos, hair still wet from the flower pot, flew over to check on Alden. Carissa watched her brush Alden's hair out of his face and give a thumbs up.

Alden would be okay.

The door swung open. Carissa recoiled, but it was only Reg and Cameron. Reg grinned and twirled a skillet in his hand.

"You won't have to worry about any more kelpies." He walked in without seeming to realize what he was seeing at first, then he stopped as if an idea had hit him square in the nose. "What happened here?"

Cameron, who also wielded a cast iron weapon, dropped the pan he was holding and helped Alden stand.

"They nearly drained me. Chaos, too."

"Why?" Reg asked.

"They're taking as much power as they can."

"How did they catch you?" Cameron asked.

"I went to see Jane and at the ship, but the Ocean Reaper was there instead. Did he get her?"

Carissa assured him she was fine. Then, she embraced Cameron and said to Reg, "So, you got the kelpie?"

"A few whacks with these did the trick," Reg said.

"He's out cold on the kitchen floor," Cameron added.

"And O'Mally?"

"Gone," Raven said from the doorway.

She walked into the room with an impatience. Chaos didn't go to her this time. Raven didn't seem to notice.

"Holly and Barnaby are helping the dazed tylwyth teg. I think they knocked the sense out of her—or she's just a strange one. And there's a kelpie you two gentlemen will have to carry out of here."

"I'm not sure we can. He's twice our size put together," Cameron said.

"I've got this one." Reg pulled a small packet out of his shirt pocket.

It was presumably MacLir's magic.

"I'll help," Alden volunteered now that he was growing stronger.

As Raven and the others left the room, Chaos tugged on Carissa's ear. She didn't mind it as much this time. She stopped and looked in the direction Chaos was pointing, which was the birdcage this time.

"What is it?" Carissa asked.

Chaos flew behind the cage. Carissa followed. There, sitting on the table, was a book. It had no jacket cover and no discernable writing on the front. The pages looked old and worn. Carissa picked it up and opened it to the title page. Unlike the dust jacket in the Moss Hill Library, the title on this page was entirely legible: *Spells and Incantations of the Druid Order of Queen Maeve.*

Chapter 18

Kelpie Kidnapper

Chaos argued but eventually agreed to see Hiya and Cynth home. She pushed her friends off of the road to the straightest path possible. Even though she promised to stay with Nan, Carissa knew she'd zip right back to Vale the moment the sprites were safe. Carissa hoped they wouldn't be in Vale that long.

It was already dark when they met Varick and Jane on the road.

"Where's Warren?" Raven asked.

Jane cradled her arm. "I don't know. Something pushed me down and he was taken. I think, I know it wasn't—Alden!"

She ran to her brother the moment she saw him. Alden hugged his sister, asking if she was all right. The scene annoyed Raven. Carissa understood her well enough by now that in the midst of a battle, displays of emotion were a bothersome interruption.

Carissa asked Varick even before Raven. "What did Jane mean? Did she see an ankou?"

"If it was, it was too quick for me to see it. Though I was somewhat distracted at the time," Varick said.

"With what?" Raven asked sharply.

Varick sneered. "There were humans, though not Mossies, gathering all around the town. Every visitor on the island must have gotten word about faeries. My guards were reporting to me in intervals all night about the human invasion."

"Jones," Carissa said. "We shouldn't have trusted Belkin to keep her quiet."

"Or it might have been Haley. And I was worried about warning *her*," Reg said.

"Did they get in?" Cameron asked.

"No sidhe guard would ever let that happen. Vale is safe. They've gone with the sun."

"So has Warren. We have to find him," Jane said.

Varick clenched his jaw. "Yes, we swept the area, but we had no luck."

Still standing beside her brother, Jane said, "Perhaps it was the same person who attacked the captain."

"Guys, this guy is really heavy, even with your magic, Reg," Cameron said.

"Oh, all right," Raven muttered. "Varick, take them to the sidhe mounds and put him in a cell. Do not question him until Carissa and I return."

"If the attacker is the Ocean Reaper," Reg began.

"Then we'll have to be creative in catching him," Raven finished.

Cameron shifted the kelpie-man between Reg and Varick. Once free of him, he made his way to Carissa's side. He waved Alden closer.

"No, Carissa told me about this Ocean Reaper. Alden and I are coming, too. You're going to need an ankou if you're going up against him."

"*You* can come along and get yourself killed if you want," Raven said to Cameron. To Varick, she said, "The ankou doesn't leave your sight. Put him in a cell if you have to."

"What has he done wrong?" Jane balled her fists.

With her soft voice, she didn't seem very intimidating. This was as close to anger as she ever seemed to get. Carissa wondered how she would ever frighten off unseelie fae with a demeanor like that.

Raven rolled her eyes. "He hasn't done wrong, he is a liability. The reaper or the changeling or whoever is after him wanted him for a reason."

"Then he and I will go home. Our family magic can protect him, both Morgan and Macara said our home was under enough spells to keep us safe."

"Oh, all right, but go already. Come on, Carissa." Raven walked away like she could not be bothered to stay a second longer.

"You'll be all right?" Cameron touched Carissa's arm.

She leaned into him, then nudged him with her shoulder.

"Go, I'll be fine," she said.

Before going separate ways, Cameron whispered to Carissa, "If it really is an Ocean Reaper, don't rush into danger. Even if he gets away, he's not worth your life."

Carissa and Raven wandered down the empty streets of Vale alone. Carissa's parents' home was not far away, and briefly she thought of checking in on them to see they were all right, but Raven would probably be against it. Besides that, if they knew she was chasing an Ocean Reaper, they'd probably insist on coming with her.

"Here, I hear something," Raven ran back toward the way they'd come.

Carissa's stomach twisted. It was also the direction of her parents' home. Was she right that her parents had been targeted?

Carissa felt relieved when Raven turned toward the old pathway out of Vale. They'd passed close to it earlier. Briefly, she wondered if they could have passed the Ocean Reaper.

A figure came into view within a dark reddish-orange mist. Then another appeared in the unnatural air. Carissa's heart pounded as they approached.

That was, until she heard the familiar ring of her mother's voice calling out her name.

"Cari, what are you doing out here?"

Raven held her back. "What are *you* doing out here?" she asked. Once she saw who it was, even Raven dropped her guard.

Carissa's father answered, "We put a few spells on the humans. Nothing serious, just enough to make them forget why Vale woods seemed so interesting."

"Forgive the cloud, I couldn't think of a better way to spread my magic so quickly."

Orange must have been the color her mother's Tuatha de Danann magic took. Carissa had never seen her use it before. As she got closer and the fog dissipated, her mother started to use it again.

The orange mist grew from her hands as she looked past Carissa. She and Raven both spun around. Raven's own black cloud began to twist around her. There was a figure emerging from the night.

It put up its hands.

"It's only me."

Warren Druvall appeared in front of them. He was scuffed up with dirt smudges on his chin and forehead. Raven eyed him suspiciously.

"What happened?" she asked.

"It was an ankou. I'm certain now he was the Ocean Reaper."

"He let you go?" Raven questioned.

"He wasn't after me. I think he was just trying to escape the town. I got in the way. Did *you* have any luck?"

"Everyone is safe. We got the kelpie," Carissa said.

"Does Macara know you came to Vale?" Carissa's father asked.

Raven interrupted, "If we're going to catch O'Mally, we'll have to question the kelpie. Come along, Carissa."

"Raven, did you talk to Macara about this mission of yours?" Carissa's mother demanded.

Raven turned to call out behind her as she kept walking. "Tell her yourself if you must. Warren, be a dear and escort them. Carissa and I are going fishing for some answers."

***

"HER NAME IS Samantha Haley."

The kelpie, named Gerard Buxley in his human form, began his confession. He took up half the cell even when handcuffed and seated. He also looked miserable.

"That's my publisher." Reg looked confused. "She's not a fae, she's…oh. Oh no, Sam."

He looked like he'd just realized that O'Mally had taken Sam Haley's form because she had killed her. Carissa put a hand on his shoulder.

"What are you doing in Moss Hill?" Varick asked.

Gerard hesitated a moment before answering.

"Sam is a book publisher. I'm a hunter, fisherman, and survival guide. She hired me to help her on this trip." His tree-trunk-sized arms rose and fell. "It was just a simple job. Go with her to Moss Hill, explore the forest, do some hiking, keep her safe, that sort of thing."

"We know you're a kelpie," Reg said.

"Was a kelpie. All right, still am, I guess. But I left that community a long time ago. I live among humans now. Took a human name, with a surname and everything. I'm part of a fishing community in Lyme Regis."

"Why live among humans?" Carissa asked.

"Why are you in Moss Hill?" he asked in a cantankerous tone. "Think I like drowning people? Like it's a hobby?"

"You did it earlier," Cameron said.

He neighed like a horse. Carissa winced but did not step back. Cameron's arms found her shoulders. Whether it was to support her or calm himself she wasn't sure. All she knew was, it was never wise to argue with a kelpie.

Then again, this was an interrogation. "You were scared off by a sylph after pushing Miss Jones out of a window," Carissa accused in a calm, steady voice.

"I wasn't trying to kill the woman. Just scare her off. I had to get the—"

He stopped.

"The what?" Varick asked.

"It was a book, wasn't it? *Secrets of the Fae People?*" Cam asked.

"That was the first book she talked about."

"The first book?" Carissa asked.

"The first day we were here, she said she needed to find the writer of that book. She'd talked to some of the townsfolk and they said he'd be at the marina in the morning. But the morning I went to meet her, she told me she needed me to take a woman to a boat without being seen. I could sense magic on the woman, but Sam, well, I didn't think she even knew I was a kelpie until that moment. Then I found out the woman was dead. I wanted to stop, but she said she knew these powerful people who would kill...there's a girl in Lyme Regis...I don't even know if she likes me...but...."

Carissa looked at Cameron. The same compassionate look in his eyes told her that he understood what the kelpie was trying to say. O'Mally had threatened him into helping.

"What was the name of the second book she asked you to look for?" Raven's voice cut through compassionate looks like the hull of an icebreaker.

"Incantations, something. I'd know it if I saw it."

"*Spells and Incantations of the Druid Order of Queen Maeve,*" Carissa suggested.

Everyone turned to look at her. Slowly, Gerard's chin rose and fell. Raven, for the first time since she'd been in Moss Hill, looked worried. She paced back and forth while Gerard continued.

"That was it. She talked about leprechauns—first she said she just needed some kind of treasure. What do I know about leprechauns? Water fae don't care much for magic on land. I followed what she said. Then, she said she needed something in the woods, but it wasn't a treasure, it was a berry of some kind. She needed it for a potion."

"To switch magic?" Carissa asked.

"Yes."

"What did you do with this potion?" Raven asked.

"We didn't make it. We kept all the ingredients in the refrigerator on the boat."

The refrigerator. They didn't think to check there.

"Was this the same boat you were on earlier?" Warren asked.

He spooked Carissa so that she jumped. Catching Cam's arm steadied her. She let go to see that Warren had entered the brig and relieved the soldiers standing guard.

Gerard stared at Warren without speaking.

"Tell us everything and you have nothing to fear," Raven assured.

"You heard her," Warren said, "speak."

Still hesitating a moment, he answered, "Yes."

"Saturday morning."

Varick nodded. "The ones you kidnapped are annoying troublemakers, but they are people. You will be held responsible for any physical or mental harm you caused."

"Where would O'Mally, um, the woman you called Samantha, go now?" Carissa asked.

"I don't know. She doesn't tell me anything. Maybe on the boat."

"He could be lying," Cameron whispered.

"We should check the boat," Varick suggested.

"My elf guards can check the area," Warren replied.

"I'm not unseelie. If you let me go, I promise you'll never hear from me again." The kelpie looked between Warren and Raven.

"But what will the humans and kelpies hear from you?" Warren asked.

"I won't say a word, I promise."

"You won't remember, anyway."

Warren pointed the hazel wand at Gerard. Varick's hand caught his wrist.

"You do not have the authority. The elders will decide his sentence."

"If we wipe his memory, he leaves and he's no longer our concern. If we wait, humans and any unseelie he worked with may wonder why he hasn't returned on time, and our lives become even more complicated."

"He said he's not unseelie," Reg said.

"We barely questioned him. What if he remembers something else that helps us find Samantha?" Carissa asked.

Begrudgingly, Warren sheathed the wand.

"Is there anything else you have to say?" Warren asked.

Gerard covered his eyes.

"I just want to go home."

Never did a grown person with so much apparent strength seem so weak. Carissa almost wondered if Raven and Warren had scared him too much. He couldn't look the druid in the eyes for more than a few seconds, and he never even attempted to do so with Raven. It almost made Carissa want to reassure him.

"We won't get anything more from him," Warren said.

"Agreed." Varick led the way out.

"Coming?" Cameron asked.

Carissa turned to Gerard.

"The sidhe don't believe in harming humans. Any help you give us will only help your case."

He looked pitifully at Carissa.

"Unless you can keep that skeleton away from me, no one can help me."

"Who?" Carissa asked.

But Gerard looked away. Then he lay down, defeated. He wasn't answering any more questions. Cameron gently pulled her away.

When they left the brig, two soldiers passed Carissa and Cam as if they were on a mission. She would've asked what was going on, but she could piece it together based on what Warren was saying.

"I'll see to the escort personally."

"Varick will see to it he doesn't escape. You'll need to prepare your men for your journey back."

"We can't leave without O'Mally back in custody. It was my responsibility to transfer her back to Moss Hill and I have an obligation—"

"Then catch her," Raven said. "But take your orders without argument or take his place on the brig."

Raven's eyes were like fire. The reddest shade of amber glowed from her face so that any and all were shocked and compelled to follow. Warren didn't dare say a word.

Gerard was out of the brig and halfway past them when Raven's orders were given. The poor guards holding him stopped for a second before realizing that staying there was not in line with Raven's command. They resumed at once and increased speed when Raven turned and walked behind them.

Her voice resumed its usual sharpness. "Come, Carissa, let's see about this new path to Vale."

"Go," Cameron said softly. "I'll check on Reg and get Maren home."

Carissa smiled as she watched them walk away.

"Why do you suppose Raven didn't want Warren to go with them?" Maren asked Cam in a loud whisper. Or maybe Carissa's elf-ears were the only reason she'd heard her. Whether anyone else had heard her or not, it was a good question.

Chapter 19

Magic and Motives

Y ou didn't tell Raven you'd found the book?" Maren asked the next day at the apothecary shop.

Carissa was grateful for a slow day, now that fae and humans had both been affected by her parents' spell. They might remember the panic of the last few days, but more as a dream than a real occurrence.

Alone at the counter with Maren, Carissa relayed what had happened the day before. This included how she'd found the single piece of evidence that had made a Tuatha de Danann turn pale. Anything to do with Queen Maeve seemed to have that effect.

"I slipped the book to Tabitha. I'll go there later today to get it back," Carissa said.

"You think you can trust her?"

"It's Raven I don't trust. You should've seen her, Maren. She barked orders at everyone with no care of whether or not they were in danger. All she cared about was catching her targets. She didn't even show concern for Chaos. I'm beginning to understand why the opinions of her are so varied."

"I'm not sure if it's better to have her on our side or the unseelie's side," Maren said.

"She is skilled. I don't think I'd want to go up against her."

"She couldn't even catch a changeling," Maren pointed out.

"I don't think she was only fighting a changeling."

"You think the Ocean Reaper was there?"

"Do you think a changeling could subdue an ankou and fight a Tuatha de Danann alone?" Carissa asked.

"I guess not." Maren shuddered. "More powerful than an ankou—no wonder the sidhe are in a panic." She turned to Carissa. "Tell me why I shouldn't be panicking right now, too?"

"Because we all came out with no more than a few cuts and bruises. Varick has posted armed guards all around Vale—including Tabitha's. Macara and Raven went to the docks last night to retrieve all the ingredients Mrs. O'Mally had saved for a potion. And we caught the kelpie, who doesn't actually seem like an unseelie."

"All that's left is a changeling and an Ocean Reaper," Maren finished her train of thought.

"Did you find out anything from Parker that might help?"

Maren sighed for dramatic effect. "As usual, talking to him was a big disappointment. All he said was that he overhead two people talking in a spice shop in the fish market. It was a man and a woman. His description of the man was a little different than Holly's."

"How?"

"Tall and thin, well-muscled. He didn't say the man was hairy, but people see people differently. Anyway, he was sure they were the kidnappers. They were plotting to go into Vale and finish their spells. The minute they realized someone was around, they went their separate ways."

Carissa frowned. It wasn't a lot of information and nothing that was useful to them now that they knew who the kidnappers were. Maren sighed again.

"How are you after speaking to him again?"

Maren shrugged. "Fine. He's leaving today. You know, I was going to tell him off. Tell him he hurt me by being such an awful person. But then, when he said goodbye, I realized I wasn't really hurt. I knew him longer, but I didn't care about him as much as I care about Reg. I'll probably never see Parker again and I'm completely fine with letting him go. I just said goodbye too."

Carissa wrapped an arm around Maren's shoulder. "I'm proud of you," she said.

It was a relief to spend a slow hour in the apothecary shop with the usual handful of human customers. Carissa only wished there were fae customers, too. She kept one eye on the Otherworld, but Vale seemed to have continued its quarantine. They waited for news of any kind from Raven, Cam, or Reg, but no word came.

At around half past nine, the shop bell in the Otherworld rang. The door swung open and Holly bustled in. Maren, already on edge, dropped a bundle of herbs when Holly switched to the human world.

"Sorry, but I had to rush over and share the news. They found O'Mally! She was on that little ship."

"Haley's yacht?" Carissa asked.

"That's great!" Maren said. "Now, the sidhe can question her and find out about this Ocean Reaper."

"Maybe the ankou can question her, but the sidhe certainly won't be able to," Holly said.

"She's dead?" Carissa asked.

"As a dormouse."

"It's doornail," Maren corrected.

"It's both," Carissa said, quickly moving past the turns of phrase. "Now, how did she die?"

"The Ocean Reaper. Warren cornered O'Mally when she fell into the water. The waves pulled her under and when Warren tried to save her, the Ocean Reaper grabbed him by the neck—he had red marks around his throat, poor man could barely speak. Anyway, the Ocean Reaper said to Warren, "Let the sea take her.""

"Why would he do that?"

"Macara said that the Ocean Reaper must've been after O'Mally for plotting to use faerie magic. Maybe the captain had been in on it, too. Reapers, sylphs, and other fae sometimes overhear things. Now that she's gone, he'll likely go right back to the seas."

"Oh, Cari, isn't that wonderful? I mean, it's awful she's been killed, and the Ocean Reaper sounds like a nightmare to deal with, but he'll leave Moss Hill alone from now on," Maren lit up.

"Yes, that's definitely good," Carissa said.

Maren pouted. "What's wrong? You're biting that lip again, and it's making me nervous."

"Sorry," Carissa said.

"What's to be nervous about? Moss Hill is safe again."

"Yeah, of course. Just out of curiosity though, what did Raven say about it?" Carissa asked.

"Who knows with Raven. She's probably found another problem to fuss about," Holly said.

"Only there's another problem, isn't there, Carissa? Don't lie, I can see it in your face," Maren said.

"Not a problem necessarily. It just feels like it was too easy."

"That's a problem you should be happy to have," Holly said.

Carissa smiled. "Right. I'm just overthinking things, that's all. I'm glad everything has worked out."

Holly and Maren seemed satisfied with that answer. There was no use alarming them again. Part of her really wanted to believe it, too.

***

TABITHA WAS BETTER at keeping secrets than Carissa expected. She was surprised to see that when she arrived at her home, Tabitha was having afternoon tea with Raven herself. Neither of them were talking about the book.

"I came to see if this girl was all right. She had a close call yesterday, after all," Raven said, in an uncharacteristically sympathetic tone.

"I'm as right as a rainstorm," Tabitha smiled.

Raven looked incredulously at Carissa when Tabitha wasn't paying attention. Carissa wasn't here to explain correct expressions to Tabitha, and she knew full well Raven wasn't here just to check on the tylwyth teg. Taking a seat in one of the chairs beside the two women, Carissa accepted the offer of tea. She placed her bag in the empty chair.

"You take yours with sugar, don't you? Silly me, the sugar is in the other room. I'll have to go get it." Tabitha jumped to her feet, winking not so subtly at Carissa as she left the room.

Fortunately, Raven may have missed the facial expression. She hadn't missed too much else. Once Tabitha was gone, Raven let out a snort.

"Lord, that is a strange fae!"

"Why are you here?" Carissa asked.

"She's hiding something, can't you tell? I had to check it out."

"Do you think she's involved in all this somehow?"

"I always think everyone's involved until I can prove different. You'd do well to learn that as soon as possible. Or maybe you have already. Are you here to question her, too?"

Carissa knew by now that Raven sensed truths directly. So, it was best to give her an indirect answer. Picking up her sugarless teacup, Carissa blew on it to cool it down. She used the cup to cover her lips as she spoke. Raven could interpret that as keeping secrets from Tabitha.

"I thought there might be a clue here we missed."

"If there is, she's hidden it," Raven said as Tabitha reentered the room.

She was clutching a book like a tray, with the sugar bowl on top. Carissa paled. Why would she hold the book in plain sight? But Tabitha explained it away.

"Here it was, right with this old recipe book." She put the sugar on the table with one hand and held the book on her lap beneath the table with the other.

Raven rolled her eyes as if to say that they were wasting their time. She and Carissa stood up.

Tabitha, looking like she wasn't sure what was happening, stood too.

"Thank you for having us. We'll be on our way," Raven said.

"Oh, okay. Thanks for coming. Don't forget your bag, Carissa," Tabitha said with another wink Carissa hoped Raven hadn't seen.

As it was obvious to Carissa that it would be, the bag Tabitha handed her was heavier than when she'd put it down. Carissa thanked her. Then, she followed Raven out the door.

"They still have that ridiculous path to Vale the long way around," Raven said.

"Where are we go—"

Before she got the question out, Carissa found herself dizzy as she had last night. She reached for the nearest tree to lean on. If she wasn't so disoriented, she would have said something to Raven about her lack of warning before moving them through space like that.

Raven took a vial out of the lining of her blood-red jumpsuit. The potion inside of it glistened a red to match her clothes.

"Is that...?"

"I've finished the potion O'Mally was working on. Now, I just have to tell Warren and the king's men to take it to the king for safeguarding."

"You said that was an illegal spell. Why didn't you just destroy the ingredients?"

"It's illegal to procure the ingredients—draining an ankou, using a nature faerie, and stealing leprechaun magic—but that was already done. It seemed a shame to waste it. Besides, if the other side is seeking such powerful spells, we ought to have as many as we can on our side."

Carissa clenched her teeth. If she thought speaking to Raven would make her realize how her actions were wrong, she would have. She would have liked better to scold her. But Raven might react badly to that. Raven was already walking away when Carissa finally snapped out of her thoughts.

The sidhe guards at the redwood stepped aside for Raven. Just inside the entrance, she spoke with one of the sidhe elders for what felt like forever while Carissa waited. She caught sight of Macara exiting one room and walking toward another. Macara stopped upon seeing her.

"Carissa? Why are you here?"

"Raven brought me, though I'm not sure why I was needed here."

"Has she told you anything yet?"

Define anything, Carissa thought. But then she remembered what Jane had said. Macara and Raven had been busy in Vale this whole week planning something. Carissa had no idea what. She shook her head.

Macara waved her toward the room she'd just been in. Carissa joined her. She'd never been in this part of the redwood before—or any part other than the council chambers. Then, she'd been too scared awaiting judgment that she hadn't really noticed the beauty of the rooms.

This one was warped but polished. It almost seemed like the wood was stone, petrified. If it was any place but Vale, she might have thought that impossible for a living tree, but here was the proof all around her. Hanging from the wall were mirrors, at least twenty of them. No, not mirrors.

They were portals to places around the world.

"You can travel anywhere with these?"

Macara bordered between confused and chiding. "Instantaneous travel is unstable magic. It's really only possible using the world beyond as a shortcut, and that is not a shortcut the living should want to take. No, it's like your…computer screens, I'm sure is what you call them."

Only these were far more advanced. Carissa thought the comparison ill-fitting. There was no camera adjustment, no pixilation, nothing to suggest a digital display. It was as real as an open window she could step right through.

"We've been negotiating with other fae."

"Video conferencing?"

"If you say so."

Video conferencing was definitely the wrong term. Macara pressed one display and it enlarged to become a 3D hologram of the place. She did the same with several others.

The first was a desert-like landscape with bulbous trees like the dragon's blood her parents had brought as a present to the royals in December. The second was a rocky, frozen tundra with hints of green beneath. The third a sandy bay stretching into bluer than blue waters.

"Socotra, Kerguelen, Bermeja, and several other fae communities have banded together thanks to your parents' ambassadorial roles. The leaders of each community must agree on how to deal with the unseelie."

"Have they agreed on something?"

"Just today."

"There you are, you found Macara. Have you shown her what she needed to see?" Raven appeared in the doorway.

Macara said, "You're never patient, sister." She took hold of Carissa's shoulders. "In another week or so, we'll have everything planned and you'll have a choice to make."

"About leaving Moss Hill to do what my mother did?"

"About choosing for Moss Hill and yourself the best possible future."

Chapter 20

Over Hill and Vale

The last debate of the mayoral election was held the same Saturday as Warren's ship was due to leave. The captain seemed to have recovered. Mossies and several fae of Vale overcame any remaining fear and came together to hear the debate. This time it was held indoors in the Moss Hill Library. Residents of the island only were allowed to attend.

Cameron began with excellent points about his views on commerce and trade. His "Happy as a Larke" campaign became about celebrating the wonders of life in Moss Hill. Carissa watched his parents' proud expressions as he concluded.

"Moss Hill is not isolated from the world. It is two worlds in one. I hope that most Mossies agree with me when I say I'd rather have a happy life in Moss Hill than all the money, magic, or mayhem that the rest of the world can offer."

The crowd, including Cameron's parents, clapped. Carissa could not have been prouder. Maren leaned in close.

"Cam's speech was so moving! I hope Reg does as well."

Carissa smiled, but her whole body tensed. Reg took Cameron's place on the floor. Unfolding a set of papers and pushing his glasses up the bridge of his nose, he adjusted the microphone. With the bookcases behind him, he looked like a college professor.

He pointed to a Cameron's banner as if tutoring them on the meaning of the slogan.

"Happy as a Larke has two meanings. The first is to be blissful, the second to be blissfully unaware. My opponent, Cameron Larke, would absolutely do his best to keep Moss Hill a joyful place. But he would also keep you unaware."

He gave a pained look to Carissa, but he kept talking in the same vein.

"Nearly a year ago, Carissa Shae received a letter warning about danger coming to Moss Hill. She showed this note to Cameron Larke but waited months before giving the letter to the sidhe guard. She and Cameron never told the Mossies about this note. Now, it's fitting that Cameron is campaigning to keep you all *'Happy as a Larke.'"*

Maren reddened and whispered, "I didn't know he was going to do this, I swear."

Reg pointed to a sign on the left side of the bookcases. It read in large red letters: *Over Hill and Vale.*

"Mossies, you've already faced danger. And I hope you understand by now that there is no danger you cannot overcome together with the people of Vale. With my campaign, I am promising that I will be fair and open with both Moss Hill and Vale. I know you might think Moss Hill comes first, and I know I'm not running for mayor of Vale, but I have heard from MacLir himself that this island was meant to be one town and somehow it split in two. The first mayor watched over Moss Hill and Vale together, which is why, I think, no unseelie dared to invade it in those days.

"But in the spirit of honesty, there is another reason the unseelie are here. The spell that kept us hidden from the world has been lifted. Mayor Belkin tried and failed to incorporate us into the rest of the world.

"MacLir is offering you a chance to decide: Let me help you be the first step in uniting humans and fae here in Moss Hill as an example for the rest of the hidden islands across the world, or let Cameron Larke help you stay hidden for one generation more before the Tuatha de Danann require a complete break between humans and the faerie people. We will know by your vote what you decide."

There was a clamor of rising voices by the time he stepped away from the podium. Mr. Greer tried to announce that the speeches were over. Anything by way of questions and answers was met with no comment from Cameron and a written statement from Reg that was available at the information desk. Mossies rushed between the desk and their own gossiping neighbors.

Maren marched over to Reg like she was going to give him a piece of her mind. Carissa found Cameron strangely calm as he took her hand and walked over to his opponent. Reg held up his hands.

"I know, I know, I'm sorry. But—"

"How could you!" Maren said. "You know Carissa and Cameron were just protecting Moss Hill."

"And MacLir wants the same," Reg said.

"Why you? Why did MacLir share all that knowledge about the fae with you and not just share it with a Mossie like Cameron instead?" Carissa asked.

She didn't mean to be hurtful, but it was honest to how she felt in the moment. Cameron was a Mossie. Reg was not. Why would MacLir think he was better suited to be mayor of Moss Hill than Cameron?

He shrugged. "You're right, I'm not a Mossie. I don't know why MacLir wants me specifically in this position, but I do know that I just want to help Moss Hill.

"You and Maren, you're so lucky you were born here. A magical island with fae friends and neighbors. Do you know what it's like to be raised by a founding lawyer of one of the largest firms in London? Life is a series of fact and conversations are inquisitions. My father had no sense of wonder for things you couldn't count."

"What about your mother?" Cameron asked with more compassion than Carissa could manage in the moment.

"She passed away when he was young," Maren answered for him.

Reg put his arm around Maren. She didn't pull away.

He continued, "I had nannies. Nanny Mooney was the one who taught me about the fae. She used to tell me the folk tales from her hometown in the Republic of Ireland. Father discouraged it as flights of fancy and hogwash. When I got a book deal, that was the first time he showed me any modicum of respect. I didn't write it for him, but publishing it was my way of showing him that I was doing something of value.

"What I didn't understand was that there isn't anything that I could do that would ever really earn his pride. Money is all he respects. He immediately wanted to take control of the book, negotiate for more, take over the project, come here and set up cameras all over the island."

He faced Carissa and Cameron with pleading eyes. "I said no. I didn't want to exploit Moss Hill and I didn't want to build my life around money. That's when I met MacLir and he offered me a chance to have something I actually do want."

"What's that?" Maren asked.

"What I really want, all I've ever really wanted, is to be a Mossie."

Applauses erupted from all around the room.

Pink hues highlighted Reg's cheeks. He shifted nervously, not having realized that other Mossies had been listening.

"Here, here," Mr. Burrows said.

"Here, here," Cameron clasped Reg by the shoulder. He added, "Let the best man win."

***

"CAMERON IS A gentleman," Nan said later while making tea at home.

"Gentleman or not, Reg said some terrible things at that debate."

"Terrible and true."

"Nan!"

Nan patted one end of the table and Carissa sat at the chair there. Setting two cups down, she poured tea in each one from the kettle. Then she took a seat as well.

"What I see is a man pushed into a position he thinks he wants because of his parents."

"What do you mean?" Carissa slid her cup closer. Spicy citrus filled her nostrils with a strong, zesty scent.

"Cameron's parents are doctors. And not just any doctors, his father runs the local hospital. He doesn't want to follow in his father's footsteps, but he doesn't know what he wants. So, he takes an odd job with the mayor and what's the highest position he can get working for mayor?"

"The mayor's own job, I guess. But Cameron did want this position."

"If he wanted it, he'd be mad he lost it. So, was he?"

"He was…quiet. I thought he was disappointed."

"You thought he was being a gentleman."

"You just agreed that he was one!"

"Being a gentleman means more than just being polite. It means taking the time for measured thought and realizing what the right thing to do is when a situation changes."

"What's the right thing to do here?"

"He has to figure out what he really wants and fight for it."

"Really, Nan. Fighting isn't so gentlemanly."

"That depends on what you're fighting for. Speaking of which, did you ever figure out what O'Mally was trying to do?"

"Parker said O'Mally was after a spell to save her husband."

"We're getting information from Parker now?"

Carissa's lips tightened. She didn't want to tell Nan about her deal with Parker. She hoped giving him the two spells this morning would not prove disastrous one day. But, he did give the promised pieces of intel. The last was perhaps the most interesting.

"He shared a cell with O'Mally briefly. During the first journey to Moss Hill, she said she had a powerful friend who could free Parker if he agreed to kidnap Holly and Barnaby. But, Parker that realized he would only be recaptured, and O'Mally was unstable. He told her he didn't know where the book was, except that it was printed by Kelsey and Addington Press."

"He's the one who contacted Haley?"

"Or at least made the connection for O'Mally and whoever O'Mally was working with."

"The kelpie or the reaper?"

"Only an Ocean Reaper would be powerful enough to break Parker off the king's ship."

"A brave fae to make a deal with a reaper. I don't think I know a fae who would do that—before you," said Nan.

Carissa sighed, "Grief makes one do strange things."

Nan nodded and sipped her tea while staring at the table. Chaos looked at Nan with distressed eyes. Carissa knew Nan was thinking about her husband, Carissa's grandfather.

"Are you alright?" she started, but Nan interrupted. "Is there any spell like that in the book you found at Tabitha's?"

"It's full of spells, but nothing was marked specifically. And they're not listed by category. I'm still combing through it with Chaos."

Hearing that, Chaos perked her head up. She grabbed Carissa's pinky and flew toward the sitting room. Nan and Carissa both stood up to follow.

"Looks like she found something," Nan said.

"I hope so," Carissa replied.

Chaos had been going through the book for days, with and without Hiya and Cynth's "help." Though, their version of helping was to distract Chaos from the task altogether. The nature faerie focused as she led them to the coffee table in the sitting room, where the book lay open to a page toward the middle of the text.

"What is it?" Nan asked.

Carissa read, *"Control of the World Beyond."*

"Looks like Parker was right about her motivations," Nan said.

Carissa sat on the sofa and read the spell aloud,

> *"To bring the world beyond into your will,*
> *Use faerie dust on an enchanted quill.*
> *To write your wish upon a clover leaf,*
> *Picked from a holy ground of pure belief.*
> *With ink, a potion of the sacred sweet,*
> *Leprechaun luck, rare spice, and bittersweet.*
> *The touch of magic drained from an ankou,*
> *Of life and death, the power lies with you."*

Faerie dust, leprechaun luck, ankou magic, this was definitely the spell O'Mally was using. She set the book down and paced back and forth. It was all coming together.

"This is it. I think this spell was in Reg's book, too, only without the instructions and warnings. Leprechaun luck, an ankou, faerie dust, those are all ingredients she was collecting. The fact that Barnaby said the woman smelled like honey only shows she had already purchased the 'sacred sweet.' And she wasn't at the fair to fill out raffle cards, she was picking the clover leaves. Even the berries Timmy drew, bittersweet nightshade, it was all for the potion."

"All right, so this is the spell. Why did she want to use it?"

"Her husband passed away years ago. She probably wanted to resurrect him."

Carissa continued pacing. Mr. O'Mally had died years ago. If she'd already known about the spell, she would have used it back then. Instead, she went to Tir-Na-Nog and then came back intending to use the spells. Why go to Tir-Na-Nog at all? Was there someone there who had tipped her off? If so, how did *they* know about the book and the spell?

Her tenth time pacing, Carissa noticed Nan's fingers tracing the spell in the book. Chaos floated over Nan's head, smoothing Nan's hair with her hands in a comforting gesture. Carissa sat back down beside her.

"Nan?"

"I can understand how she was feeling. To bring the ones you love back to life, that would be a temptation."

She put her arms around her grandmother and squeezed. Nan patted her arm. They sat like that a moment.

"I would have liked to know him, too," Carissa finally whispered.

Nan said, "I'm not just talking about your grandfather. When you live as long as I have, you see everyone you know pass before you. I've lost so many friends and family. I had a sister once. Now she's gone, too."

Carissa didn't know what to say.

Words felt inadequate. With grief, words always felt like a Band-Aid over a deep cut. They might cover the surface, but the healing had to happen on its own. And when it was done, a scar would still remain.

Pulling out of the embrace to sit up straight, Nan said, "Never mind, now we know O'Mally's motive. At least we can lay this mystery to rest."

Carissa wasn't so sure. This wasn't a spell just to bring someone back to life. This was to control the whole of the world beyond. O'Mally might have just had her husband's resurrection in mind, but who would want to have full control over life and death? Even ankous didn't have that power.

Then it hit her. O'Mally wasn't the only one involved. Parker's description of the man with O'Mally at the fish market differed from the accounts of the kelpie because it wasn't Gerard. She knew exactly who it was, —once she realized who had purchased the rare spices needed for the spell—and now was the last chance she had to confront him.

Nan rose from the sofa. Chaos hovered to the blinds. The nature faerie pulled on the strings to open them wide. Nan gave a concerned glance out the window.

"Looks like that storm Raven Corvus promised us is here."

As Nan walked away, Carissa asked chaos to summon Alden. He appeared instantly, breathing heavily and holding his hands closed in two fists. One was red with a tinge of blood on the corner. Chaos hovered right up to his nose to see what was wrong.

"What happened?" Carissa asked.

Alden opened his palms, gesturing as if in argument, "She's going with him! She says she loves him—she's known him three days."

"Wait, Jane is leaving with Warren?" she guessed.

He nodded. "She's under some kind of spell. I don't know how to break it and I can't fight Warren in front of Jane. I tried."

He grabbed his reddened hand and rubbed. Carissa stepped forward to wrap it. He stepped back.

"It'll heal faster than a human's. What am I going to do?"

"I called you here because I need you to take us to the Marina. The captain may be able to detain Warren."

"You knew he enchanted Jane?"

"It's worse than that. Warren is not what he seems."

Chapter 21

Tempest Tossed

Nan was right. A storm was forming overhead when she arrived in the marina. The tempest waited long enough for Carissa to make it to the ramp of the ship. The moment she was safely on the dock, Carissa stopped Alden from going any farther.

"Go get Macara. Tell her to meet me on the king's ship along with the sidhe guard."

"Just Macara?" he asked.

Carissa looked at Chaos. The sprite grimaced. Carissa could think of several different reasons not to call on Raven, but she was powerful.

"We may need as many people as you can find. If I'm right, the Ocean Reaper is still in Moss Hill, and he's responsible for more than just O'Mally's death."

Carissa raced up the ramp to the ship of the King of Sidhe and Elves. In the rippling water, the boat and the ramp leading to the deck rocked back and forth.

Carissa struggled to keep her balance, holding the rope in the stormy weather.

Up higher was a figure in a black, metallic corset and black pants. It was Raven, dressed for war. Carissa called out to her, and she spun around.

"What are you doing here?"

Carissa competed with the wind to shout her response, "On the boat, when you first met Warren, you asked him if he was the ankou—"

She was cut off by elf guards who surrounded them. The guards eased when their captain appeared.

"My lady Raven, what can we do for you?"

Raven looked at Carissa. "I'm sure you were about to give an excellent summary, though I'm a little busy to hear it just now."

Captain Heurle said, "With respect, I would like to hear what she has to say."

"Oh, be quick about it, then," Raven tugged at her collar and sleeves like she'd wasted perfectly good spy apparel.

"Warren attacked you, Captain. He was working with O'Mally. They were trying to get to the ankou, Alden, to drain his magic to use in a potion. Warren knew if he killed you, Alden would appear. When that didn't work, he used Alden's sister to lure him to their parents' home. Now, he's hoping he can get away and take her with him.

"See, Warren isn't who he seems to be—"

"Alright, that's enough," Raven said. "They get the idea. Now, captain, get the brig ready with spells powerful enough to hold the Ocean Reaper and we will go catch one."

Carissa followed Raven to the same cabin they'd seen him in a day ago. To Carissa's surprise, Jane was there as well. She had not expected to see Warren lying on the bed with Jane tending to the injury he'd received at Alden's hand.

"Lady Raven, Carissa," he croaked.

"Warren," Raven said. "Jane, run along home. I have some business with the druid."

Warren took Jane's hand. Jane smiled at him, then stood and faced Raven.

"I'm leaving with Warren. This is the life I want, and Warren has helped me see that it's a life I can have."

Raven ignored Jane. "Warren, let go of her."

Jane's eyes fell on Carissa. "You want to be the protector of Moss Hill. If I leave, I can take your place and speak to the Tuatha de Danann. We don't have to do what we don't want."

Carissa shook her head. "I didn't want to be Moss Hill's protector—not at first. And maybe I don't want to travel, but I won't know that until I try. Why don't we try our roles, Jane? Then we'll know what we really want for ourselves."

Jane sat back beside Warren and stared into his eyes. "I know what I want for myself."

Chaos flew around Jane, trying to get a better look at her face.

"It's no use," Raven said. "She's not herself."

"Jane is coming off this ship, and you are under arrest, Warren Durvall."

Jane stood like a puppet as Warren sat up. She pointed her hazel wand at Raven, whose arms were poised to attack her as well. Carissa tried again.

"Jane, you're under a spell. You don't want to fight us."

But Jane was already firing off a blast of white light in their direction. Raven blocked it easily, but the goal was accomplished. Warren ran out of the cabin and disappeared.

Without thinking, Carissa fled the room to chase after him. Chaos flew with her. Carissa heard the door shut behind her and saw Raven sealing it with her magic. At least Jane would be safely locked in a room by herself, but already she was pounding on it from the other side. Jane wasn't Carissa's main concern at the moment. As she raced out to the main deck, Chaos clung to Carissa's hair and hit right into her shoulder when Carissa stopped abruptly.

Warren stood in a menacing stance on the upper deck. Raven pointed her fingers at him, ready to shoot magic in his direction. Chaos posed herself in much the same way on Carissa's shoulder.

Carissa said, "Careful! He's not just a druid, he's the Ocean Reaper."

As if to prove his words were true, Warren took on his full reaper form. He looked down at both of them with white eyes. His body was draped in a silver cloak. His face was a skeleton. As many times as Carissa had seen Alden, he was nowhere near as frightening in form.

Before Raven could fire, Warren struck. A billowing cloud of charcoal and fire-red enveloped them. Raven rushed in front of Carissa before they both flew black. It took a minute to struggle against the boat's violent rocking for her to catch the railing and pull herself onto her feet. Except for some bruises, she was unharmed. The smoke hadn't cleared, but she could feel right away that Chaos was no longer with her.

"Chaos? Raven, where are you?" Carissa shouted.

Raven, having borne the brunt of the magic, lay at the very head of the boat on the floor. Chaos zapped her with her faerie dust. She did so once more before Carissa made it to them.

"Enough with the CPR! I'm alive."

Raven was already starting to sit up. Carissa and Chaos both held a hand out to Raven. She eyed them before begrudgingly accepting help.

"I would've had him if it wasn't for you distracting me," she said, even as she grunted in pain while Carissa pulled her to standing.

"Never mind that, he's on the run. Alden went for help. Macara should be here soon."

"I don't need Macara. I can perfectly take care of one druid ankou myself."

Carissa rolled her eyes and followed Raven. If the three sisters could have learned to work together, she wondered if Miss Morgan would still be alive. Raven stopped.

"Look."

Carissa peered over the ship's railing. There, running down the pier, was Warren.

"He's going for the other boat!" Carissa shouted.

She ran ahead of Raven. The few guards who had remained on the ship were now coming out of the main cabin. Raven shouted orders.

"You five at the bow, and you three at the stern. You there, link your magic and keep the boat in place. The reaper may try to move it."

Carissa could hear the frenzy of feet clamoring behind her. She raced down the ramp and onto the pier. Turning behind her, she saw that Raven had gone.

Chaos tugged at her shirt. Carissa looked in the direction the sprite was pointing to see movement and glowing lights on the shore. Varick and his guards had arrived, but it would take time for them to make it past the sand to where Carissa stood.

An explosion at sea caused Carissa to bend at the knees. She squatted and clutched her ears. Turning and rising, she saw flames in the marina.

It could only be one thing.

The cruiser yacht had exploded.

Two figures appeared on the dock. Warren flew backward, sliding past Carissa. Raven took to the sky. A large gust of black clouds mixed overhead.

Warren tried to stand. A dark figure took him down from behind. Carissa squinted in the rain to see Varick and Warren locked into a fight. The waves grew fiercer with every blow. This reaper was the stronger of the two with his control of the sea.

The king's ship knocked into the pier. Varick jolted to the floor. Jane appeared at the base of the ramp.

"Warren!" she called out.

Warren locked eyes with Jane. Varick lashed out protectively, but Warren reached out with his left hand and pulled Varick down the pier with an invisible force. Before he was thrust into the water, Varick was wrapped in a white light. He froze mid-air.

"No!" Jane's arms had reflexively shot toward Varick. There was no longer any wand in her hand, but the white light was hers. Keeping the magic steady from her fingers to Varick's form, Jane shouted, "Leave him alone!"

The sky darkened. Warren's grip broke. Varick fell back onto the pier; he was shaken but not hurt.

Jane's hands still glowed with druid magic. Her eyes were wet with tears visible even in the now drizzling rain. Warren shifted to human form.

"Jane," he said. "You and I, we could be amazing together."

Jane shook, visibly struggling against Warren's spell. She took a resistant step toward him. Chaos flew between them, holding one arm out on either side as if to say "stop." As if Chaos had called on him, Alden appeared by Jane's side. Carissa advanced.

"You're a reaper. You're not alive to be in love," Carissa said. "But you want to live again. What's more, you want a spell that gives you power over life and death. You manipulated O'Mally by saying you would bring her husband back to life. Then, you pretended you were attacked by the Ocean Reaper so that you could, as the king's druid, receive the potion and use it on yourself."

Even in the darkness and intensifying rain, the forms of several sidhe guards emerged from the beach. Alden stepped in front of his sister. Thunder drew their attention upward. A twister spun overhead worse than the one Raven had come to Moss Hill in.

In response, Warren called on the sea to show its wrath. Every ship in the marina knocked violently against the docks. A wave washed over her high enough for Carissa to hold on to the pilings so she wouldn't be swept out to sea. Chaos held her hands out as if pushing the ship back. It was a good idea. Carissa called on every part of her magic to steady the weather before it turned into a hurricane. The waves seemed to slow.

Something threw her forward. She skidded. For a moment, all her senses could process was cold wood on her skin, water splashing as her hair whipped across her face and the distant shout of "Carissa!" in a male voice.

Cameron's voice, she realized as she came to a stop. When she'd recovered her senses enough to stand, she could see Macara bringing the sea and the weather to a calm.

Warren tried to disrupt the clouds with the magic from his hazel wand, but each beam that came out of it hit like a firefly battling a thunderstorm.

Cameron ran up behind Warren, shouting, "Now, Reg!" He skidded the last few steps and ducked. Reg threw some sort of vial in the reaper's direction.

Warren pulled water from the ocean and used it to swoosh away the vial. It fell into the water without so much as a splash. The distraction gave Carissa enough time to physically ram Warren to the ground. She yelled to Cameron and Reg.

"Back to shore now!"

A pinkish hue began at Carissa's hands. She was ready to fight Warren as he returned to standing, but Alden intervened. He appeared by her side and grabbed her wrist just in time to transport her to the beach. Carissa let out a frustrated cry. She felt a bit like Raven for having been interrupted in her fight.

Alden rested a calming hand on her shoulder. "Raven will take out the whole pier."

As if on command, a large center section of the structure collapsed.

"I have to get my sister." Alden disappeared.

Now Carissa could hear Varick shouting orders to call everyone back. When the smoke cleared, Warren was pinned between Raven and Macara's magic. A mix of purple and black swirled around him.

"I have him handled."

"If you did, you wouldn't have damaged the pier," Macara said.

"Let him go and do something about this weather," Raven ordered.

Carissa looked at Jane. As if they had the same thought, they both ran forward. Carissa could hear Cameron and Reg trudging through the wet sand behind them.

When they made it close enough, Carissa touched the water and Jane reached up to the sky near where Raven's magic had formed. The ocean calmed, the rain stopped, and clouds parted.

Macara let go of Warren. She folded her arms and raised an eyebrow at Raven.

With a smirk, she said, "I told you they were ready to begin their roles."

"I never argued with you on that point."

Warren struggled against Raven's magic. With the two sisters fighting, it appeared he might have a chance to loosen the bonds. Chaos threw something at Warren. It was the vial. Apparently, it hadn't splashed into the water because Chaos had gotten hold of it first.

Macara put a handout and drew it toward herself before it hit its target. Chaos kicked the air and argued in her sign language way. Macara waved a finger.

"Not a great idea, unless you want an even bigger explosion. Those bonds already have Raven's and my magic."

"Uh, I'll take that," Reg said. "Don't want MacLir's power in risky hands. No offense, Chaos."

"The potion!" Carissa realized it was still in Warren's possession. "We have to get it back."

Raven laughed. "Do you think I would have given the real potion to him? No, that's safely tucked away with me."

"Maybe you should give it to the Sidhe Council," Reg suggested.

Raven glared. "MacLir may have given you some power, but you do not—"

"Raven," Macara put an arm around her sister, keeping her from scaring Reg into even paler shades. "Stop scaring humans and help me repair the damage."

The sidhe guards began leading Warren away. Jane stopped in front of them, blocking their path. She stepped closer to Warren to show the last bit of feeling that remained in her heart for him. It took the form of a slap.

Then, she linked hands with Varick and walked away. Cameron gave a that-has-to-hurt look before reaching out for Carissa. She reached to take his hand when Warren called out her name. She turned back to see him grinning.

"I have a message for you from Niall Shae."

The guards looked to Carissa for a sign as to whether they should let him speak or continue to drag him away. She searched her memory for the name. Niall Shae. That was her cousin—the descendent of Maeve she'd never met who posed the greatest threat to Moss Hill. Carissa gestured for the guards to let him speak.

"There will be schools of kelpies, flocks of sylphs, and scores of other fae ready to destroy Moss Hill if the island doesn't surrender."

"Niall never be able to destroy Moss Hill," Carissa responded.

"Destroying Moss Hill is not what he wants. He wants a prosperous town. He wants every town on earth to be like Moss Hill. A world of peaceful co-existence between fae and human. Join him and help make that world come true."

"If that were all he wanted, he wouldn't have had to make threats. He would wait out the experiment to prove to the Tuatha de Danann that humans and fae can live together in peace."

"But is Moss Hill in peace? You have two towns here, not one. Which of the fae live among humans? Brownies, gnomes, disgraced leprechauns, a few of the weaker elves. Not the strongest of the fae. They know that humans would fear them. And do the humans of Moss Hill really accept the fae?"

Carissa thought back on Mrs. Larke's statements at Saturday's luncheon. She resented being stuck in Moss Hill. She wanted Cameron to move on from the town. But that was economics, wasn't it? It wasn't that the fae were holding them back, it was protecting the secret of the fae required some holding back from the rest of the world. It certainly wasn't because she feared them.

Warren went on, "The humans can't handle knowledge of the fae. They fear anything they don't understand. They'll try to destroy the sidhe and elves. And they'll lose because seelie and unseelie both are more powerful than a human."

"So, the role of the humans in your idea of Moss Hill would be to serve the fae?"

"My idea is that the Tuatha de Danann would bring peace to the whole world."

"You are human, Warren. You're discounting yourself in this new world. Will you also be a servant?" she tried to reason.

"I already serve the Tuatha de Danann. But I am not human. I am the Ocean Reaper."

"You were a druid, Warren. And druids may have some sidhe blood, but they are human, too. Maybe you forgot that when you became the ankou of the ocean, but you're serving the wrong side."

"My captain, general, and leader is and always will be Niall Shae." He raised his voice for Macara and Raven to hear. "He would welcome any Tuatha de Danann to our cause. Join us, and I would also be glad to call you my superior."

"You'd take orders from me?" Carissa crossed her arms.

"Of course."

"Fine, then give up being a reaper and go to the world beyond in peace."

Warren smiled. "Until you side with Niall, you're my enemy, not my superior."

"It was worth a try."

"It is a good idea, though," Raven said. "Alden, you go along with the sidhe guards and escort Warren back to Vale."

Alden looked at Varick, who waved them onward. Warren did not resist as Alden led him back to Vale. Carissa stopped Varick.

"Two ankous in Vale? Are you sure the fae can handle that?"

"They'll understand that one of the ankous is not for us to fear," Varick assured.

Jane smiled at her brother. "They'll have to see you for what you are."

She held Varick's hand as they walked away. Carissa felt the tension of the fight ease away as she watched them go. Maybe Jane was beginning to see Varick for what he was to her now, too. Chaos flew overhead, dropping heart-shaped faerie dust above their heads.

Carissa laughed, then leaned into Cameron for a kiss.

"Ready to leave?" he asked.

"One minute. Wait for me," she said.

She walked to Macara, who was repairing the pier with Raven's help. Raven grumbled something about the task. Carissa didn't imagine Raven was used to cleaning up the aftermath of her battles.

"Will you move on now?" Carissa asked Raven.

"Yes and no. There's still the matter of what I came here to do," Raven said.

"What's that?"

Macara was the one who spoke. "Meet us here tomorrow after the voting. All your questions will be answered."

Raven agreed. "Even ones you didn't know you had."

Chapter 22

A Proposal

The mayoral candidates and their supporters gathered together in the Second Street Pub to hear the results of the election. Friendly chatter filled the restaurant until the results came in, then everyone quieted, and the television above the bar was turned up. The graphics showed the final tally while the announcer called it.

"What an election this has been. With the article by Tilly Brier explaining Sean Belkin's reason for dropping the race, and with our newcomer's eye-opening speech—and, of course, a brilliant job of our interim mayor—it was an intriguing series of twists and turns. But it ends early this morning with a close call victory for Reginald Smith.

Cameron held out a friendly hand.

"Congratulations," he said.

"No hard feelings?"

"None at all," Cameron said.

Reporters swooped in to take pictures of the candidates' polite exchange.

Reg let out what sounded like a sigh of relief and reached for Cam's hand. "Good, because now more than ever, we'll need an ambassador to Vale."

"I may need a little time to think about that." Cam clapped Reg on the back lightly and let go of the handshake.

Carissa and Maren stepped up to join them. Maren gave Reg a hug, and he walked to the podium. Cam took Carissa's hand, intertwining his fingers with hers. She wrapped her arm around his while Reg gave his acceptance speech.

"Thank you, Mossies, for the honor, more than anything, of allowing me to be one of you."

He continued in a joyful tone, but Carissa wasn't listening. She could feel a change in Cam. He stood tall and was smiling, same as always, but his grasp on her had strengthened. She almost sensed that his mind was more focused than it had been in months. He clapped at the end. Carissa did, too.

As soon as the speech was over, he retook Carissa's fingers and led her outside. They walked down to the beach. Finally, they found a bench and sat, watching the ocean.

"Are you going to be fine with this?"

Cameron breathed in and smiled as he exhaled. "You know, I think I'm better than fine."

He took Carissa's hand.

"I think I might actually prefer staying in the role of ambassador to Vale."

"Really? Why's that?"

"This wasn't me. Being mayor might've been more living up to my parents' expectations. Turns out even that didn't please them."

"I think they just want you to be safe."

"Really? Seems more like they want me to be Charlie. But that's beside the point. Do you know what I was thinking when I saw that Reg was going to win and they announced him mayor?"

"What?"

"I felt like it was a new beginning. A chance to choose what I really want instead of what I think I want."

"And what is it you want?"

"'To live in a place where there are no secrets, everyone is a friend and you can spend a lifetime with the people you love.'"

He quoted her statement from the lunch with Cam's parents. Then he left the bench to kneel on the floor. He took her hands into his own.

"I was going to do this on Valentine's Day, but I wasn't sure we were ready."

"And you think we are now?" Carissa asked.

"Aren't we?"

She answered by pulling her hands away. She turned his right hand over and held it in her hands. Cameron's eyebrows pulled together as he searched her face. They twisted into utter confusion as she took the ring she'd given him days ago and slid it off his right hand.

"This was my grandfather's wedding ring. I was hoping one day you'd want to wear it like this."

Understanding washed over his face as she slid it on to his left hand.

He answered by sliding the Claddagh ring off of Carissa's right hand and on to her left, with the heart also facing out. The rings signified their engagement.

They sealed it with a kiss.

"Oh, that's beautiful." Tabitha rushed in to hug them both.

The whole of their friends and family had somehow gathered around them without their noticing. Carissa laughed and embraced Barnaby as he held back tears.

"Back to the pub to celebrate, drinks are on me!" Clancy said.

Emony glared. Clancy put a hand on his heart. The other he held up like he was swearing before a jury. "That just means I'm paying for a round. I won't have any myself, I swear."

Maren and Holly immediately started planning out venues. They'd be arguing before the night was out.

Chaos pulled Carissa and Cameron away from everyone. Raven and Macara were standing on the edge of the beach close to the water.

"A happy engagement to both of you," Macara congratulated.

"Terrible timing," Raven said. "Or good, depending on your perspective."

Carissa and Cameron looked at each other and back at Raven.

"I suppose it's time to reveal my real purpose in coming here."

"Why do I have a feeling I'm not going to like this?" Carissa asked.

Macara put a hand on Carissa's shoulder and squeezed. "I'm sorry. If there was any other way…."

"Sorry? About what? You're going on the adventure of a lifetime!" Raven said.

Chaos danced in the air and settled on the top of Carissa's head. Raven hooked Carissa's arm with her own. She led Carissa down the shoreline. Macara "tsked" and stepped in time with them. Cameron took giant strides to keep up. Maren grabbed Reg's arm and ran behind.

"Wait for us!" she called out.

Closer to shore, the still water became ripples, then waves as the thunderous sound of horses rose above the waves.

"Stay back, they're kelpies!" Reg shouted.

"Oh hush, these are good ones." Raven waved.

The white horses dipped their heads as if bowing and stayed in the water where the waves were thin and unthreatening. Behind them, a beauty of a boat rose out of the ocean. Its wooden veneer shone so brightly at first Carissa thought she was looking at gold. The protective barrier of magic that must have kept the air inside it while underwater burst like a bubble. The waves became gentler until the boat swayed back and forth like a bassinet rocking a baby.

Reg walked ahead of where Carissa had stopped and took off his hat to stare in wonder at the sight. His voice full of reverence, he named the vessel as he recognized it—"the *Scuabtuinne*."

"What's the *Scuabtuinne*?" Maren asked behind them.

Reg turned around. "Is...is he on the boat?"

"Is who on the boat? What's the *Scuabtuinne*?" Maren demanded this time.

"Long ago, MacLir had a boat that he had crafted with a great deal of magic from all kinds of fae. He gave it as a gift to his adoptive son, Lugh," Raven explained.

"He goes by Logan now," Macara added.

"You, Carissa, will travel on this boat to the Island of Hy Brasil to meet with the Tuatha de Danann yourself and make a case for Moss Hill."

"Me? Why would they want to hear from me? Haven't you spoken to them?"

"They didn't want to hear from my sister," Raven said.

Macara rolled her eyes. "I made the mistake of using you as an example. Your courage and love for humans and fae was my proof that a future with all people on earth was possible."

"Now they want to hear a plan from you about how to reveal the fae to the rest of the world," Raven said.

"What? I don't have a plan." Carissa felt herself growing hot. Her elf-light flowed under her skin as her heart began to race. Raven seemed amused.

"Look, her face is matching her hair. I think she's turning tomato-like. I've seen humans do that before. Curious thing, isn't it."

"That's anger, Raven, and Tuatha de Danann can feel it, too," Macara said.

"Do they? I don't think I have before. I've seen it on the battlefield, though, when a warrior goes into a rage. Are you going into a rage, my dear?"

Carissa didn't quite rage, but she did say with a little more fire than usual. "Aren't you supposed to be the ones who decide on things like that? I can't make a decision that affects the whole world!"

Cameron stepped between Carissa and Raven. In classic politician mode, he raised his arms and spoke calmly.

"I'm sure Raven doesn't mean to put this all on you, Carissa. You and Macara have thought about a plan, haven't you?"

"What do you think we've been doing all this time?"

"A few weeks to decide the future of earth?"

"We've been considering this for centuries," Macara explained. "We've been negotiating with the king for the last few months and the Sidhe Council these last few weeks. Trust us, Carissa. We'll tell you what we've decided so you'll be prepared. All you have to do is tell the Tuatha de Danann your input on our plan and convince them that the world is ready for this."

"And if I think it's not?"

"Then the Moss Hill experiment will end. The doors between worlds will forever close, and you will have to choose between worlds."

"Wait—choose?" Maren asked. "You'd make Carissa choose between her parents, Sal, Hela, all of them, and...us?"

She looked at Carissa. Her brows wrapped her eyes in concern as they swelled with tears. Cameron's arms embraced her.

"She can't make a choice like that. I would never want her to," Cameron said.

"Neither would we, but I'm afraid the agreement was made before she was born. She must merge all worlds or choose between them."

"She must merge all worlds? Of course!" Reg's eyes lit up. "You'd need all three types of magic to open the portals forever! That's why the decision has to be now or never. At least now or the next time a person is born with your particular—"

"Reg, get to the point," Cameron said.

"Don't you see? When Carissa's grandfather founded Moss Hill, he knew it would only be a matter of time before someone was born who was of all three worlds. Carissa is that person—her grandfather was a Tuatha de Danann, her grandmother was human, and when their daughter married an elf, she became all three: Tuatha de Danann, human, and fae."

"Wait, but you said you need all three types of magic. Humans don't have magic," Maren said.

"Druids do," Carissa clarified.

"All humans do, technically, but it's only the druids who know how it works. Some people think there's an element of genetics—with things like psychic ability running in families. No one has been able to prove that."

"So if I have all three—"

"Your magic could essentially merge all realms."

"It's a nice theory, and it's true to some extent, but that was not your grandfather's intention," Macara said.

"We didn't know a child would be born like Carissa. We thought a druid, a human, and a Tuatha de Danann would work together. It's really better than one person alone," Raven explained.

"When you were born, we did our best to hide you from the unseelie so they couldn't use you to open the portals," Macara added.

"They would never be able to do it on their own. They'll never succeed in anything, anyway. There's too much hatred between them for them not to destroy themselves in the process," Raven said.

"My readers will hear about this!" a voice rose in the marina. Early as it was, Miss Jones was already out on the docks. She wasn't the only one. Mossies and tourists began to spill over from the hotel and the shops just opening for the day.

"I saw those shape-shifting horse creatures in the water! Don't deny it! And what about that ship? I saw it rise from the water like a submarine, but it's an open sailing yacht!

"You've been keeping this secret right under our noses as if we were blind? This affects the whole world! You can't keep a secret like this forever."

"Carissa, why don't you do the honors?" Raven whispered.

Carissa walked toward Miss Jones and put a hand over her eyes. People tried to shield their faces from a ridiculously pink, ominous cloud that was either magic or a gas of some kind filling the air. When they realized the mist would overcome all of them, a few of the tourists tried to run. Then, confused, they stopped and scratched their heads.

Carissa put her hands down.

"Nothing to worry about. Just a high tide shaking everything up. That's right, you had a great time on this island, and now you're going home."

Miss Jones struggled against the amnesia. "No, I won't let you hide this. You and your faerie people are putting the whole world in danger! I have to tell everyone."

The spell would catch hold of her eventually. One day, she wouldn't erase memories from outsiders. She hoped one day there wouldn't be outsiders—just one happy world of human and Mossies.

Maren nonchalantly offered her hand for Miss Jones to shake.

"Miss Jones, it's that attitude that makes you a star reporter. Thank you for your diligent reporting."

Confused, Jones shook her hand and mumbled something like "don't mention it" before scratching her head and wandering toward the ferry boat. Carissa felt a little like Raven, knowing things that others didn't and guiding them to just the right actions. She hoped this wouldn't become a habit, and yet, if she was perfectly honest with herself, it felt good.

"Safe journey," Maren called out.

"That wraps that one up nicely. So, what do you say, Carissa?" Raven asked.

Chaos floated overhead, settled on Carissa's shoulder, and gave her a thumbs up. Taking his hand, Carissa looked at Cameron questioningly. He gently squeezed her fingers and gave her a smile. She turned her attention back to Raven.

"Yes, I think I'm ready for a little adventure."

Want more great content?

Hi, I'm Astoria Wright, the author of The Faerie Apothecary Cozy Mysteries. I hope you've enjoyed the first book in this series.

Check out the rest of
The Faerie Apothecary Mysteries:

Chaos in the Countryside – A Novella Prequel
Book 1: *Herbs and Homicide*
Book 2: *Remedy and Ruins*
Book 3: *Elixirs and Elves*
Book 4: *Charms and Changelings*
Book 5: *Potions and Panic*
Book 6: *Talismans and Turmoil*
Book 7: *Tonics and Turning Points*

To keep up to date about this series and others by the author, check out the website:

www.astoriawright.com

Sign up for the mailing list for updates and freebies available only to members!

Thanks for reading!